The Butts

The Butts

Driss Chraïbi

(Les Boucs)

Translated from the French by Hugh A. Harter

Robert Hayward Professor
Ohio Wesleyan University

Three Continents Press, Inc.
Washington, D.C.

ISBN: 0-89410-324-5
ISBN: 0-89410-325-3 (pbk)
LC No: 83-70251

Originally published as *Les Boucs,*

Cover Art by Mike Allen

Three Continents Press, Inc.
1346 Connecticut Avenue N.W., Washington, D.C. 20036

TABLE OF CONTENTS

Driss Chraibi

Photograph © Seuil

Germaine Bree on Chraibi

It was in the mid-fifties that the name of Driss Chraibi, a young Moroccan writer, first became known in French literary circles. Those were years of ferment that preceded the phasing out of French Rule and the long drawn-out Algerian War. The young French-speaking Muslims, educated in French schools and newly attuned to French culture were caught up in the cross currents of conflicting and violent emotions. These erupted in a flow of highly articulate literary works, novels in general, most of them clearly autobiographical which though originating in Morocco, Algeria, and Tunisia, were written in French and published in Paris. Widely read in French-speaking countries, they have not, with rare exceptions, been translated. Professor Hugh A. Harter's translation of two of Chraibi's many novels is therefore all the more valuable and the first, it is to be hoped, of many others.

The choice of *The Butts* and *Mother Comes of Age* for Three Continents' first publications of Chraibi is a happy one: *The Butts* is Chraibi's second novel. Like the first, *Le passé simple,* it is marked by violence, excess, a coruscating love of rare, rich words, ellipses of all kinds. Like its predecessor, it speaks of revolt. But whereas in *Le passé simple* the revolt was directed against the oppressive customs of Islam, incarnated in the father, in *The Butts* Chraibi excoriates the dehumanizing treatment meted out to the "Arabs" or "Bicots" in the slums of a Parisian no-man's land. To translate *The Butts* is a difficult enterprise. Hugh Harter, experienced translator that he is, has succeeded in maintaining the chaotic vigor of the gifted but still inexperienced young writer.

Between this early novel and *Mother Comes of Age* stretch some fifteen years of experience as a novelist. Much had changed, politically, in those fifteen years. Morocco had been an independent kingdom since 1956; a new world had "come of age," combining the modern with the traditional. The later novel is entirely different in mood: restrained, humorous, tender. Here the translator faced another difficulty: how to catch the tone in English without falling into the overly sentimental. The story of a Muslim woman's liberation, through the gentle but determined action of her two sons, is moving. Chraibi's writing sometimes comes perilously close to an emotionally colored didacticism. What saves it is a humor which can be translated only if the human context within the Moroccan cultural situation is fully grasped. This takes imagination, knowledge, and taste, besides the gift of language. Hugh Harter's translation is richly endowed with all these.

Translator's Introduction

Driss Chraibi's first novel was a bombshell. It effectively launched its author on a long and successful writing career, but somehow that first work, *Le passé simple,* published in 1954, has dominated critical thinking about Chraibi's work. It has persistently projected an image of the author as a rebel caught in a web of violence and verbal destructiveness. As more and more full-length novels appear, we can see that there is far more to Chraibi's work than violence. There is also tenderness, a marvelous sense of humor, warmth, and deep human concern. The early works barely reflect this, but it is important to remember that as we read the novels that set Chraibi on his fictional journey. In a sense, both the first and the second novel are acts of parturition as the protagonists of these works engage in a searing search for identity and personal dignity. They are both odysseys, the first divorcing the central figure from his native culture, and the second, a journey of alienation and deep disillusionment.

In *Le passé simple,* the protagonist's name is Driss Ferdi. It is not hard to identify him, in part at least, with Driss Chraibi. Both the fictional and the real man were born in Morocco into a well-to-do middle-class family of traditional Islamic background, both were educated in a French *lycée,* being taught the French language and French culture, and both became rebels against the culture of their family and native land. Both Drisses struggle to free themselves from the strictures of a repressive and patriarchal society, and both leave Morocco in search of a new life in the country of their adopted ways. Driss Ferdi's father embodies the authority, the ignorance and the superstition of Islamic traditionalism, while France represents a hope for freedom, justice, and equality. Ferdi embraced French ways with enthusiasm, and he leaves for France at the end of the novel full of expectation.

By the time that Chraibi's second novel, *Les boucs* (*The Butts*), was published in 1955, the long, brutal and divisive Algerian War was under way. This perhaps explains why the work's protagonist, Yalaan Waldik, is an Algerian in France rather than a Moroccan. Nevertheless, we must see in Waldik a kind of extension of Driss Ferdi, the young man who departed for French shores full of illusions about finding a new and better life.

The novel opens on a note of violence and of bitterness that is sustained throughout its length. In this work, however, the author's reaction is not against the Islamic world, but against France, against the Occidental world that has promised so much and delivered so little. Waldik encounters rejection and hatred rather than fraternal acceptance. He speaks French, but he is not French, and the figure that most fully epitomizes this, the author-publisher Mac O'Mac, makes this brutally clear to Yalaan in his condescention and callousness toward him.

Chraibi is venting his spleen in his devastating portrait of Mac O'Mac, and makes little bones about his feelings toward some—at least—of the publishers in France with whom he has worked. This raises, of course, the question of the extent to which this novel, like Chraibi's first, is autobiographical. Undoubtedly to a fairly large degree. As with Driss Ferdi, Waldik's experiences reflect his creator's tribulations. Chraibi left Morocco in 1945 at the end of World War II, but it took more than a decade of wandering throughout Europe and trying himself in various skills before he came to his true calling, that of writer.

Yalaan Waldik, whose name signifies "may he who sired you be damned," is also an aspiring writer. The story he is determined to tell is about the suffering and disillusionment that he and his fellow "Norafs" have undergone in the land of plenty to which they have so naively migrated. His book is entitled "Les boucs," the "Scapegoats," or "Butts" of a country that recruited them and execrates them. Yalaan is their self-appointed soul and their spokesman, as Chraibi becomes with the publication of this second novel. We know that Chraibi has long resided in France and sired two families there; he has earned himself a lasting literary reputation, but being as sensitive as he is, he must have undergone much the same searing and cruel experience that he ascribes to his fictional hero and his long struggle to find himself a publisher that would give both to his work and to himself a renewed sense of worth and a recovery from his "ego failure."

The Yalaan that we first see is steeped in hatred and bitterness. His companion is a kind of alter ego, a kind of Sancho Panza to the Quixotic Waldik who refuses to face reality or to be defeated in his quest. The friend's name is Rauss, so called from the German word "raus," the order for "to get out" that he had learned during his imprisonment in a Nazi SS concentration camp. At the book's beginning, Rauss kicks open the door of the house where Yalaan is sitting despondently and throws him a raw and bleeding leg of mutton. Rauss had stolen it for his friend from a French butchershop. Outside the house the sky is a mournful gray. It and the howling wind set a tone for the mood of the novel, as does the violent "overture" with its description of raw meat, the slow and passionless strangling by Yalaan of his pet cat, or the reminiscence of the "banquet" of mice and rats, fried in their own grease and flavored with shallots, that Rauss and Waldik have shared.

Yalaan is sitting in a little shack in Villejuif, a grimy suburb to the south of Paris. He has just served a prison term and has come back to the house in which he lives with a French woman named Simone. He has had a son by her, but the child only adds to the sordid misery of the father; Patrice, as the boy is named, has meningitis and must be taken from his shabby crib to the hospital. Simone shares her house and her bed with Yalaan, and she partakes of his misery, his madness, and his apathy. She is devoid of feeling except for her hatred of Rauss. She has lost shame and fear, and has sunk ever more completely into the morass of sordidness that envelopes her, to the consternation of the "Christians" who live in the shacks nearby hers.

The love that she and Yalaan share is based on "raw sex, hunger, and anguish," but even Waldik cannot understand why this young and basically attractive woman would share his abject poverty and his despair. Yalaan delights in the sensuality of tormenting Simone who, for her part, accepts her role with a terror tinged with sexuality.

Rage seems to give Yalaan an identity, and Rauss and Simone's attachment to Waldik bestow an individuality on them. The Butts of the title of the book, however, do not possess even that shred of human dignity and particularity. They are indistinguishable, a band of "non-men" stripped of all semblance to humanity like the inmates of concentration camps.

Chraibi reinforces his image of them by portraying them as totally mechanical, a machine-like group when we first see them marching single file along the streets like a string of lifeless puppets, ragged and dirty, one like the other, equal in their misery and their rags. They have even lost those dubious affirmations of existence, the French identity and unemployment cards, conferred on them at one time by a cruelly indifferent but exacting bureaucracy. They desparately turn to crime to better their lot. To no avail: the police refuse to put them in the prison which comes to represent stability and security, and assured food and lodging. They are "worked over" and shoved into the street.

Somehow they still cling to an illogical hope for work. As we first see them, they are marching through the winter's cold, all twenty-two of them, to apply for a job as diggers. The corporal, their leader who deciphered the sign announcing the work, pleads with the contractor to give the Butts a chance to show how hard-working they are. The contractor rejects them. He wants no dirty Arabs working for him. Late that night, the police find his body with twenty-two knife wounds in it lying in the shack where the Butts had gone in vain. The Butts had vented their fury, but their lot does not change. Their future will continue with the hypnotic monotony of nothingness.

It is only at the end of the book, as a kind of epitaph, that we see the little shoeshine boy mesmerized by the idea of a bright and certain future for himself. It is a French priest who plants that hope, one of the "missionaries of materialism and of the machine gun . . . specialists in everything from zero to human dignity."

● ● ●

The Butts, Chraibi tells us, belong to those beings caught in the cogs of history, those persons "in all times and all places . . . and not just North Africans in France—whose fate it was to be sacrificial victims, whether the Negro in America, the Jew in the Middle East, the Moslem in India, the slaves of ancient Rome or Greece, assimilated into a civilization, as though to prove that no creation of man has ever been for everyone or ever been perfect."

Waldik lives with the Butts, but he is not one of them. He is separated from them by the abyss of his consciousness. He is "an Arab who wants to write books," but he is also the little Berber boy who came to France to find work, and who found no work, no lodging, no help and no fraternity, only "copper tags and forms to fill out and unemployment cards and promises. Nothing else." He is the Arab who has learned the Frenchman's language, but who, as Mac O'Mac points out, is not a by-product of the centuries "of civilizing process" that supposedly he and Simone are. His thinking is Arabic: "I'll never live except in the absurd. For ten years now my brain, my Arab brain thinking in Arabic, has been grinding away at European concepts, in such an absurd way it transforms them into gall and even the brain gets sick from it."

In part, Waldik is representative; he shares in an experience common to the North African coming to France in search of work. What Chraibi describes is not a social tract, of course, but the scenes of life of the Arab worker in France is, sadly enough, a true one. We know that from newspaper and magazine accounts that have appeared with regularity in France as crime, hatred and prejudice have again and again reared their ugly heads. These episodes parallel to a striking degree the exploitation and degradation of migrant workers in our own country.

None of Waldik's memories are pleasant. Working in a mine, he was given the most remote and darkest areas to dig because he was not a member of the union. He and his fellow Noraf miners reach out for companionship with their French co-workers without success. They watch their counterparts go off to wife, home and family while they go off to their solitary misery, mitigated only by the alcohol that is sold to them at exhorbitant prices by an old man bent on extorting them. Drunkenness is their refuge from their sordid surroundings. Only Waldik has a goal. He wants to buy a radio, but the money he so painstakingly saves is stolen from its hiding place beneath the floor of the shack he shared with the other Norafs. There is no honor, even among thieves. Arab exploits Arab. The innocent Yalaan, when he first arrives in France, is stripped of all of his possessions by the Arab hangers-on in the French reception center. Later on he pays excessive rent to an Arab "landlord" who provides him and his fellow "inmates" with a dirty mattress in a filthy basement whose only light is provided now and then by a single electric bulb. Every inch of space is utilized in an insane parody of "civilized" living.

Waldik almost becomes a total victim. He tries to commit suicide. He speaks of himself as though he were not himself: ". . . a North African named Waldik had existed, had wanted to play Ghandi or Tarzan in Europe, and had ended up swallowing five grams of sleeping pills." But once he has passed through this nadir, he will survive and eventually triumph, as his book will be published and the story of the Butts will be given to the public to judge.

Yalaan is undoubtedly the central figure of the novel. He is also the most fully fleshed-out and realized. With one exception, we might say that he is the only character that acquires real life. The exception is Isabelle, the other mistress who had found Waldik wandering drunk in the street. She too is an outcast, a kind of human derelict, a war-child whose health has been forever undermined by the privations of the Nazi Occupation. Despite this, "she believed in the goodness and fundamental vitality of man." She is a survivor, and she acts as a kind of conscience for us as well as for Yalaan. She condemns the exploitation of the Arabs by Europeans, but she blames them as willing victims. As she puts it, "you have always let yourselves be exploited. Long before the French got to you, you were nothing more than bastards that everybody passed from one to the other, generation after generation, century after century, like a plot of ground: Phoenicians, Greeks, Romans, Visigoths, Vandals, Arabs, Turks, French . . ."

She does not spare Yalaan either. She tells him: "Your misery is of the soul. No Frenchman, and no sum total of history created it in you. It comes from you alone. You will die with it. You live more a prisoner of it than in any jail, more sadistically than in a hairshirt, and oh, so very contented! When I picked you up in the street, I wanted only to see the man in you. I picked up a piece of rag, and now I'm throwing that rag away."

Isabelle instinctively and automatically becomes a part of the Butts. She shares with them their primal response to the song of the thrush and the coming of springtime. She joins their pagan dance of joy and shares the meager meal of roasted sheep, along with ". . . instinctively going back in time to the source of creation to become again plain creatures of God in a natural state of creature, hibernating in winter, being reborn in spring, stealing their food, with rusty shacks for a lodging, with a language that expressed their needs and their instincts, static like their truck garage or Rauss's jalopy, with no evolution except the aging of cells, killing all hope in them, the pure and chimerial creation that man only created because he wanted to go beyond his condition as a creature, and thus become a misfit on earth."

Man is the misfit on earth, but Yalaan is a misfit among men. He belongs to no group or society. In him we see the clash of two worlds, of Orient and Occident, or more precisely, of two theologies, that of Islam and that of Materialistic Progress. In him we can also identify the fundamental problem of our epoch, the cancerous atrophy of spiritual growth in our times that engenders the anguish and alienation of the displaced Waldik who flounders in the tortures of consciousness. He is the agnostic who remembers faith, but who cannot recapture it. He has left a world that he cannot fully reject and that reaches out in memory to haunt him. He has entered another world, but cannot be assimilated into it. He is the ultimate refugee; he is the intellectual and spiritual nomad who belongs to no one and nothing. Even his "cause," the Butts and the North Africans like them, is alien to him.

In Chraibi's latest two works, *Une enquête au pays* and *La mère du printemps,* published respectively in 1981 and 1982, he seems to have resolved Yalaan's spiritual problem. The central figures of these novels are, like the Butts of the scenes of the rites of spring, primal creatures rooted in the simplest and most enduring values of human co-habitation, respect, hospitality for the needy wanderer, the dignity of the individual, prudence in the absolving of one's needs, and a wisdom that cuts through the veils of materialism as well as of dogma. Chraibi, like Yalaan, writes like a prophet of old. He condemns, but he searches. He is a conscience that seeks to warn us against the prestidigitations of progress and technological magic. Yalaan's misery does eventually lead to insight, as has Chraibi's. *The Butts* describes a significant segment of that journey.

PART ONE

COPYRIGHT

1

> In recent years psychiatry has
> moved more and more in the direction
> of a concept of *ego* failure as
> the basis of mental disorder, and herein
> lies real hope for scientific advance.
>
> Ward C. Halstead,
> *Brain and Intelligence*

Of wood. Of white wood. This is a chair of white wood.

Someone kicked open the door. I saw a foot, long and narrow, and shod with a heavy cowhide shoe. He stamped the cement floor so hard that the sound reverberated through the room like a pistol shot. Then he stuck the point of his foot in the cat's belly, and I saw the cat's tail whirl through the air. His heel slammed the door shut.

"So here's the meat."

The mutton hit the wall and left a red mark. It bounced against my feet with a little squishing sound.

"The butcher said to me, and for you sir, what'll it be? I said to him, I want that piece of meat over there. I gave him a good one with my fist and took the meat."

The celluloid ticket with the price on it was still attached—in red numbers: 840. I took it off and stuck it to my lapel with the vague idea that one day I'd have 840 francs to go to pay the butcher. My gestures were slow and distracted.

"He must have called the police to give them a description of the thief: North African. They sure got him too, the North African, any one, the first one that came around the corner. And the butcher identified him: No doubt about it. That's the one."

I sat down and looked at him. I looked at him with terror. Like a blind man who is suddenly given the eyes of a lynx.

The windowpanes are gray on gray mornings. Outside, the trees are like black skeletons. I watched them turn in the wind, and I heard the wind. I had recovered my sense of sound also. But in a vague sort of way, without any real sense of timbre or of pitch, and I said, as I listened to the moaning of the wind, that it was the neighing of a horse.

"We have to cook the meat," said Rauss.

He was standing there. He hadn't moved since he walked in. Massive. With hollow cheeks, and the sole of his shoe—the same one that had kicked the door open and shut—stamped on the door. In a little while (I know he's hidden under the stove) I'll put the cat out by the tail. He has very little time to live.

"What tree shall I cut down? We've got to cook this meat."

The other one, the one down below, he could die too. But he wasn't cold, for now at least. I had gone down and stuffed his crib with rags and sacks. He let me tuck them in without a sound, without a smile. He has a fever of a hundred and four.

"The plum tree? It hasn't produced anything for two years. And even if it had, what does a lousy Arab like me need with plums?"

I'm still watching. Still listening. And my fear is to act on it. If I did it, I'd go back to prison. The air of freedom, a sun's ray, what used to be, that could have been my *me,* but those are things we have to consider quietly, timidly, without haste or intensity. Only my fingers opened up, crunched, and closed again.

"So? What about the plum tree?"

I got up and walked over to Rauss, over to the door he was leaning against.

Was it my eyes? A moment later, and I saw nothing but a naked door.

I pulled it down on myself, destroyed.

I sat down again. On my white wooden chair. If it had been of teak or of raphia, it wouldn't have lasted any longer than this one. All combustible.

The windowpanes had become a sort of eyeglass, gigantic and distorting. But they kept their mournful gray. Or, could it be that I'm not yet awake? The image they give me of the outside world is like a figure out of a ballet. The leaden sky and the trees resonant—that is the backdrop scenery. I'd swear by my dog of a life and by my life of a lousy Arab that there was a crazy marionette moving out there. The legs are too long. The gestures are controlled. Sometimes at the end of the leap, the legs join the branches of the trees against the horizon. And I must admit that after all, it was just a question of a few branches that were more frenetic than the others.

Rauss, outside, was kicking the door to pieces.

He has only his shoes to break it into kindling. As far away as Bicetre, not a single Christian who would lend us an ax or a saw.

All he has to cook his piece of meat is that door. In the house, not another door except the outside one is left. The others went to the end of the garden a long time ago. A little pile of ashes, or what is left of them: the wind.

I would have liked to please Rauss. To tell him to cut down the plum tree. But Simone loves her trees. That's one of the reasons Rauss detests her.

I hear him outside, spitting, coughing, swearing. We've got the same thick hide. Thick and bitter from hatred. Neither one of us knows the real nature of that hatred. Not even who it is we hate. I distractedly picked up the piece of meat and distractedly began to knead it.

I can hear the wood crackling and groaning under his feet. I'm the one who's groaning or Rauss is the one who's crackling. Our souls are bleeding here in France.

Skin that has become ashes of skin, that too. So apathetic that the hair has refused, psychologically, to grow on it for a long , long time. They were so attractive in their bournouses and riding on their camels, a worker-priest said to me. I didn't even answer him. I don't know how to answer an insult.

Rauss came in and threw down his armload of wood. I waited for him to leave. I looked up at him. He was staring at my fingers. Between them a little dab of red minced meat squished up.

Five fingers. Rauss had skinned the mutton leg down to the hoof. The skin came off easily. The toes were like crab claws someone had quickly smashed. He did not say a word, and I heard him go out. I didn't even shrug my shoulders. I knew that sooner or later he'd come back and eat his meat—close to the child that was dying. And, no doubt—I've taken all my possibilities into account, Fabrice, and I have no choice but to accept the fact that you are dying, Fabrice—curl up at the foot of your crib and sleep the good sleep of the lousy Arab. I'm sick of it—let me alone—you need a bit of everything to make up a world . . . but what world and what life?

I was fascinated with my fingers. They were still all sticky with meat, and I opened and closed them right under the cat's nose. The smell of blood brought him running. While he was licking my hand, not a single hair on his back stood up. There was no need for his instinct to react. Or was it because—give me something to eat and strangle me afterwards—a savage hunger had reduced him to a cat's caress?

A clock began to strike. I counted the first strokes and paid no attention to the ones that followed. Nine thirty. So what? The cat had to be killed. A poor man's cat is a luxury. A poor man's charity. For two years I'd fed him with dried peas, promises and caresses. He was perfectly content with that. Until his ribs stuck out—but what of that? Someplace, there are cats with flesh on their bones.

I loved him above all for his companionship. In this lost corner of Villejuif just south of Paris, there were thirty-two shacks around mine. Thirty-two families that never said a word to me. And my cat, his guts twisted from hunger and his skin raw, never once stole a thing from them. I squeezed his throat a little tighter.

The mist began to thicken, clouding over the windows. I felt a draft, cold and feeble, sweep across the floor. I accepted the cold and the mist. The clock struck again. As if all concept of reality, every perceptible object, had to be rediscovered. In the drama.

Mice? Rauss had chased some down and skinned fourteen of them. And a couple of rats. Certainly not for the cat. The stomach of a lousy Arab digests mice and rats.

I remember that banquet of rats. Pan-fried in their own grease and seasoned with shallots. Only Simone turned green. I never reproached her for that. She isn't as strong as we are. That night she went to eat corned beef and cabbage at the Josephs'. One of the thirty-two families that live here. Their door is always open to her. With a lot of contempt, a lot of misunderstanding, and a dose of Christian charity, they would say, one day that North African will kill you, dear.

I loosened my fingers, caressed the cat's back and then scratched his stomach. I knew my eyes were like two slits. Like the eyes of the cat that did not go away. If I had been in his place, I'd have jumped like the Word of God when my hand touched him. He purred softly and looked at me affectionately. In the fireplace the wind was howling savagely.

I scratched his head, then an ear. He moved caressingly underneath my hand, as if he had lost all sense of instinct. Neither passive nor servile, but a noble litigant: I know you're going to strangle me, but let me love you until then. A head and an ear that followed the rhythm of my caresses, ugly yellow-gray fur. I gave him little taps on the stomach, as ugly as the rest of him, and he got up and stretched. That stomach that Rauss had often kicked. Because there was only one thing in the world—and he knew it—that loved him: that cat.

The cursing of the wind, Rauss breaking up the door, had said all the insulting words a little while ago. He said them that very day, with every step he took on his long walks through Paris. Every night he snored them. I had heard them so often they were a kind of litany. Dirty Arab, said the wind, and all the other names the French used to show their scorn for us: *malfrat, arabe, crouillat, sidi, noraf . . .*

He also said: I won't work, I'll wander around, I'll steal, I'll kill . . . since the world, Europe, the Christians won't look at us dirty Arabs except through a heavy screen (that they had set up, protected with bars, and labeled: there's the Arab, the real Arab, the only one) showing up our own worst instincts, making us look at our own worst failure . . . damned Arabs, stinking Arab, filthy Afro . . . a profession of faith if you want to call it that, and why not?

Even Simone was fully aware that she was living with two filthy Arabs. With Rauss, whom she hated—can it be called hatred?—and me, by whom she had a child. Often she would light the nightlight and look at me. My God, it's not possible. Then she would turn it off. My throat would get dry. You could feel the savage inside of you. Her voice full of excuses. And I would take her in my arms, the arms of the savage, once again.

The wind was sweeping everything away. The only thing we had to keep us going was our nerves. Our only doings with the society around us took the form of curses or theft or violence that we ate slept walked saw heard lived . . . with rebellion and hatred . . . and that was the only way I loved Simone too. Even my sperm spurted hatred.

That particular morning she was waiting for me behind the gate.

"I couldn't come to the prison."

"Fabrice?" I asked. My voice was like a whine, and I heard my own saliva as I swallowed it. My eyes narrowed. A bird gave two little trills. A canary, but it might as well have been a crow.

She shrugged her shoulders and held up her arm. From where I was it blended into the garden path she was pointing to. The wind was ruffling up her dark bronzed hair. She smoothed it down with the palm of her hand and pushed a hairpin into place. She looked at me coldly. She wasn't hostile. Just detached and only vaguely interested. Later on I was to remember all of that. Mercilessly.

I got up and told the cat to stay where he was. He wanted to follow me. I stooped down and yelled at him to wait for me. He flicked his tail. I went downstairs where Rauss had a regular bonfire going. He had brought in the rest of the door and had stuffed it into the fireplace to the last scrap. He stood up and looked at me from head to toe. Twice. The fire was roaring, the walls were sweating.

"Go call an ambulance," I said.

Even before he had fully stood up, he had the posture and the presence of a hand in the air ready to slap someone.

"I know," I said. "There isn't any money for a phone call. I know. So," I shouted, "go get the ambulance on foot."

He shook himself heavily. I watched him walk through the yard like an automaton, open the gate and go on his way. I went back upstairs and sat on my chair. I wouldn't let myself look at my child.

The cat was waiting for me. I took him on my lap. When I looked at him more closely, I saw that he was even more of a skeleton, uglier and more deserving of love than ever. He even had the eyes of an ugly skeleton. He smelled of urine, moist guts, hunger, humidity, and fear. His neck was very thin. I wrapped my fingers around it until they clasped. There was still space left.

I squeezed. The fog was thick now. Grayer than the clouds had been. Mournful and fragile, thick even under my fingers. I tightened a notch. It was Simone's throat I was squeezing. I began to smile. She hadn't shown any resistance. She wouldn't resist at all. The wind gave a curse and went on its way.

I knew her to the very roots of her hair. Even her meows were a feeling of insecurity that *with the hand that is now strangling, I can, if it would give you pleasure, break off the head and throw it squirming and bloody onto the printed page.* Our love was based on raw sex, hunger, and anguish—and seven condemnations of the law against me. The law regulates life. I pressed the first phalange of my index finger against my thumb.

I smiled. Even the wind, somewhere, perhaps in the convulsing of my fingers, became a hiccup. One of those rigid smiles—I knew I was smiling with my teeth—that I did so well. I always smiled that way, a presentiment when I was about to commit a theft or attack a Christian. She hardly trembled at all. The drama, for all its theatricality, had no effect on her.

Petite, young, beautiful—I could not comprehend. My presentiment is in that hand that I was letting do its work. I could not comprehend why she had given herself to me, gotten pregnant, lived with me unmarried, in sordid poverty, the future ahead of us blocked with the rocks and cement of hatred—or why she loved me.

Not even that concept of love—like all European concepts that come in contact with an Arabo—had changed a thing inside of me, in all the four years we had lived together, in a sticky residue of madness and murder. Hunger had not penetrated a single pore of her skin. I couldn't comprehend that either.

And I couldn't comprehend why this animal, a cat—I couldn't

accept, couldn't assimilate—why . . . I had never stopped her hunger and I had done nothing to deserve her love. A few yards away from here there were always Christians and murals showing Christian meals, and Rauss beat on his stomach like the skin of a drum, and the ambulance was shrieking in the distance . . . here he was with his misery glued to mine like a moth.

I lifted him up to my eyes, hanging from my fist, by the neck—and my presentiment cried out: what you're really doing, really doing, is strangling Simone—and I yelled:

"You have epileptic fits, epileptic! . . . You've killed my son—you dirty epileptic!"

While Rauss was downstairs yelling at me to shut up, that if I didn't shut up he was going to put me into an ambulance too and ship me off to an asylum . . . But I kept on yelling, the wind had begun to croon an old Arab melody, as though it wanted to calm me down, as though it were trying to calm me down—until the cat (I called it Kitty)—not once did it try to scratch me—got too heavy for me to hold.

The noise it made when it hit the floor sounded like the kicks it used to get in the stomach. I went downstairs. The ambulance was shrieking off in the distance. I heard its siren once more. Clear, bitter, horrible. As though Fabrice, my son, had let out the cry.

Then slowly and methodically I took his crib apart, wood, mattress, covers, pillow, sheets, sacks, rags—and eyes half-closed, I started to throw them piece by piece into the fireplace where a fire straight out of hell was still ablaze.

2

> Men without conviction, emaciated and violent; men whose beliefs are shattered and whose dignity is destroyed: a whole people naked, nude inside, stripped of all culture and civilization, armed with shovels and hoes, pickaxes and hammers, chained to rusty machines, diggers of salt, sweepers of snow, mixers of cement; a people consumed with beatings, obsessed with paradise, with foods long forgotten, the intimate bite of misfortune—all of these people throughout time.
>
> David Rousset,
> *The Universe of Concentration Camps*

They walked Indian file through the foggy morning. Waves of laughter welcomed them, instinctive, quickly smothered—and afterwards you could wonder how anyone could have laughed, as if laughter had an instinctive value.

They had a heavy step, their arms just hung at their sides, and their faces were marked with fear. The people who stopped to watch them go by blinked their eyes in a moment of intense and sudden disbelief in which the conventional beginnings and ends of man were rapidly revised, and the classifications of sovereigns and metaphysics alike were brought to naught, reshuffled like a house of cards shaken to the very foundation and following through systematically. Etymologies, the sense and use of words such as human dignity, pity, Christ, democracy, love . . . They opened their eyes: the failure of civilization, if not of humanity itself, that they had seen file by dressed in rags—or at the very least, of rags stuffed with human nothingness.

Their nostrils steamed. They walked close to walls, one

following the other like fleeing rats. They came to a curb stone that jutted out like a dyke. They came to a halt, bewildered for an instant by the metallic sound of horns and brakes, the feverish step of crowds, the thousand and one little divergent signs of a life to which they did not belong. Quickly they rounded the street corner that had stopped them and returned to their familiar formation, one behind the other. But the formation again broke at every intersection, at every rough spot in the pavement, at every new road, every cross street . . . as if their stupefaction were an endless reflex, similar to bladders of dogs that let go at every lamppost on the street with one little furtive jet per stop.

There were some twenty of them. They had been walking since dawn. The rising sun had tried to find itself in them, to color them, or at least to give them contour, form, or shadow. Then the wind blew, briefly and commandingly like a policeman, determined to sweep them all away. But both attempts were in vain, for the sun was now hidden behind a mass of clouds like so many witnesses, and the wind growled. And they plodded on.

Their feet barely left the earth, as if the weight of them was conscious of these beings as potentially rich minerals, and had already bound them to the soil, wearing shoes whose soles they pretended were of leather, rubber, or even wood, but were nothing more in reality than shapes of feet cut out of old tires or metal that made a galvanized mold that bound them to the tips of their toes and mechanized their every step. They were incredible foot coverings, greased with lard or stiff with paint, looking like something void of any foot, and animated only by an ancestral habit that lifted them up and put them back down on the sidewalk in a clumsy and ridiculous fashion.

No critical perception could possibly have distinguished one of them from the other. Life had make them prisoners of their own bad humor and reduced them to an equality of misery. At one time they had had a name, a receipt for an identity card, and another for unemployment, bits of paper that bestowed on them a personality, a sufficiency and an illusion of hope. Now they were the Butts, the

Goats. No prison, no asylum, not even a Red Cross office would accept them. Day after day they did their best: robberies, knife fights, bouts of depression—which they thought, and kept on believing, could get them free bed and board. The police played their part well. They worked them over a bit, and then released them . . . But I stole something! —Go on, out! Outside! No arguments! There was even one who had been arrested by the SS and deported to a forced labor camp in Germany. He came back, smiling with all eight teeth still left, the ones that hadn't been kicked out of him, and an air of triumph and excuses: yeh, well, they didn't get any information out of me . . .

There were twenty-two of them. That day, like all the others, dawn saw them come out of their shack and urinate in a circle in the fog and cold. The Corporal had marched off at the head of the line, feeling melancholy that he was still a dirty Arabo after being in France since the year 1920, always or almost always, unemployed. Head of the line because the shack belonged to him—at least he was the one who found it, a sort of ex-garage for a Dodge truck in an open lot in the Paris district of Nanterre—and they picked up his step. The night before, by the light of a ball of tallow with a piece of wood for a wick, they had had a firm discussion. This day was not like the others.

Noon surprised them standing en masse in front of a notice board. The cold was intense, but if they were rubbing their hands, it was from pleasure. The Corporal knew how to read, and he spelled out the announcement of the placard in a loud voice, with due gravity and noddings of the head. The others repeated after him, translating into Arabic and commenting between syllables, two words laboriously put together, while they all coughed and laughed and spit on their hands, and then rubbed them together triumphantly. They understood that someone was looking for diggers, and no sooner did they get the message than the race was on, elbows and jaws banging into one another, wretched footwear slamming against the pavement and ragged clothing moving along like a line of ship's sails tattered and battered by a hurricane. There were orders and counter-orders, stops and starts in one direction and then another. But there was nothing helter-skelter about it. You would have thought that a single defection or loss of any one of them would have destroyed any chance of getting work.

The work office had closed down at noon. A notice nailed to the door clearly proclaimed it in black printed words. So they waited for two hours, silent, patient, their backs lined up against the flimsy wall of the work shack. They were like a group of the pious holding the wall upright, or like the condemned waiting for the firing squad, not shuffling a foot or so much as coughing, and even swallowing without making a sound.

A small truck backfired and braked. A man got out. Ruddy-faced, sleepy, he took them all in a single glance. Then he opened the door of the shack and slammed it behind him. Twenty-two Adam's apples bobbed, twenty-two heads turned a half circle and looked at the closed door.

"You think that's him?"

"Shut up!"

"What if it's him?"

"Shut up!"

They soon quieted down and waited. They seemed made for waiting. Their life, their destiny, their very substance was a succession of waits. They understood it very well. They had never rebelled, they had no idea of rebellion. Quite simply what for others was a profession of faith had become for them a source of unbelievable energy.

At about four o'clock, the man came out. He looked at them again with a glance of stupefaction. He seemed to think (as if given official sanction and public notice by a town crier) that his first look at them should have been enough to make them clear off.

"What the hell are you doing here?"

They understood that this was the contractor, and the Corporal went up to him. He got mad too, despite the warning that he should never get excited. Christians like calm, order, logic. A passive Arab with his glands atrophied and his soul shriveled up could be of no interest to the man whatsoever. A man living in Europe, whether a Chinaman or a Pole, was expected to fit into European ways, into

European logic and order and calm, even if someone thought it necessary for this job of digging to ask for the full story of their lives from the time of embarkation from Algiers or some other port. But the Corporal's head and bony hands began to jerk convulsively. He was screaming at the contractor. His eyes were yellow from worry, and his breath had the stink of hunger. He demanded to know if the man was the contractor himself, the person who had put up the notice about the jobs, but at the same time he tried to mollify him in case he was only an employee or a brother of the boss. Well, if that was it, no problem about it. He could finish up the arrangements in place of the head man. He and his Butts were willing to sign up with any old Christian, as long as he put a shovel, large or small, in their hands. And he went on to say that he was not hollering from anger, that he was begging him in what only sounded like anger, that he knew that the Christian (European, and what's more a contractor, a man who not only had a job himself and a purpose in life, but who could give life as well as the means to live it to other people) would surely understand.

But he didn't seem to understand anything. He just got redder and redder in the face. Finally the group surrounded him and forced him to open the door to the little wooden shack. Then they shoved him with the Corporal into the little wooden cube complete with table, chair, and telephone, whose wires they cut. They closed the door with its enameled sign: OFFICE—NO ADMITTANCE. They sat down on a pile of bricks, rusty metal, and rubbish. Through the thin partition, they could make out a muffled dialogue that they couldn't quite comprehend, that they didn't really want to listen to. The fog was getting thicker, and it was getting darker. Now and then the Corporal would open the door so they could hear for themselves. The contractor said the notice was already two days old, that he had hired some diggers, and that even if he had not done so, he wouldn't hire any damned Arabs. He sure didn't vote for the 1946 law on the status of Algeria that gave French citizenship to Algerians. Before that they had been French subjects, but with the new law, they could even come to France without a passport . . . I said to him: I'm not interested in politics. I'm hungry. I said to him: The notice is still up, so you still need workers, and a good stroke of a pick or shovel on the earth has nothing to do with race, yes, sir, and if it's a question of performance, we were ready to give a free example of what we could do . . . I said to him: Where are the diggers you hired? Show them to me. I don't see anybody working around here . . . They all shook their heads in agreement, and the Corporal closed the door again to go on with the argument.

Darkness and fog had turned the night into a kind of cold wet gray. One by one, the Butts melted into the piles of rubble they were sitting on. And a breeze sprang up, smothering the sounds of the argument that was going on inside.

It was late that night when two policemen on their nightly round went into the shack and found the body of the contractor with twenty-two knife wounds in it.

3

> He knew what this delirius crowd
> did not, what can be read in books,
> that the plague bacillus never dies
> and never disappears . . .
>
> Albert Camus,
> *The Plague*

Still now—through the painful succession, without continuity or coherence, of movement from reality to dream to the collapse of my floundering consciousness—I know with complete clarity, with a pitiless sense of details, I *knew,* as though the extraordinary tension in which I was living had projected me toward the future, that on that very night my madness had begun.

Rauss had come in, had asked about Fabrice, talked about sleep and food—not once did I open my mouth—and had then gone away mumbling about crazy people and insanity. All night I sat waiting, immobile on a chair. Fog, cold, north wind.

Early in the morning I heard someone climbing on the stairs. She opened the door, holding her purse lightly in her fingers, smiling, relaxed, with an air of physical satisfaction. She crossed the threshold, and behind her I saw the sun coming out.

"Mac's here," she said.

For a moment I realized that I was trying to smile, quickly trying to smile, a whole gamut of smiles, from triumphant to stupid, as you might try on a series of masks.

"Hurry up. He'll be here in a second."

She helped me to my feet, put down her purse, and ran her hands through my hair. Her gestures were brusque, impulsive, yet nimble. She smelled of lavender. Even if she had smelled of fuel oil, I would have said: there's fine lavender for you!

"Snap out of it . . . come on . . . don't sit there like a bump on a log . . . Here he comes . . ."

Mac O'Mac came in. Later on I was to find out: the people who strangled every bit of hope and pardoned others who believe in something, knew very well what they were doing.

"Good morning, my friend."

Energetic, assured, very informal. I have never clearly enumerated my wishes. He made a gesture toward the door, the chair. I closed the first and sat down on the second. Thank you, sir, very much. With such majesty that from that moment on I was no more than a guest in my own house. The Butts have taught me that I could never comprehend a real sense of property. Slim pickings for the man who plants in his neighbor's fields.

"I am so moved by you . . ."

"Quite so, my friend. I have studied your manuscript. Impressive. There is no such thing as inborn hate or revolt, let's be clear, nothing but basic misunderstanding—what plays on words!—misunderstanding out of which whole anthologies of revolts and hatreds are born, a lack of psychological adaptation, I would say."

I was trying to translate into Arabic, as the Butts would do. Even translated into the dialect of Algeria's Kabyle, such an explanation of their miserable existence would have overwhelmed them. They might have seen Mac O'Mac as a simple crustacean, a crab dressed up in tweed. As for me, I could play the role of questioner, factorial and transcendent because—how shall I express it?—I do understand French: I would say that Mac moved like a crab, crawling all around me, encircling me with a rigorous clarity (what is clearly conceived is clearly enunciated) and technique, down to the metal-tipped heels of his shoes that technologically tapped out commas, accent marks, and periods. Sometimes, grazing the wall, he would stretch out his arm and touch Simone on the shoulder. Everything all right, my dear? She did not avoid his touch, wasn't even bothered by it. She was sitting on the bed, watching Mac circle around as he talked, and stealthily glanced over at me.

"Because there is nothing like a different sounding of the bell to show that people, and above all, members of family, are not made to devour one another. Underneath all anger there are usually good intentions, and all hatred is definitely a misunderstanding before it becomes something else."

"I presume you're right," I said. "I think so. I believe so. But tell me, how about clearing things up? Have you read *The Butts?*"

"Why, of course I have, my friend. I spent the night reading your manuscript."

He stopped and did a gracious pirouette. Then he added—maybe he was smiling, and maybe the smile was forced—because the Arabo (that's me) would not understand a damn thing:

"And I'm sorry I did. Madame Waldik is a most charming woman!"

"I made one of those trips," said Simone as she quickly shoved a chamber pot under the bed, "that are simply exhausting! You know I had to thumb a ride all the way to . . ."

The heel taps sounded again *(de minimis no curat* Mac O'Mac). I was still capable of feeling stunned. Just then the insects showed up. Three flies out of nowhere that flew through the air like a team of oxen or a squadron of bombadiers in tight formation.

"It is possible," said Mac O'Mac. "The subtlety and reason of reasoning are not often the handmaidens of an energetic spirit. The proper impetus of a work owes a great deal to the impetus—often quite wrongly—of one's character."

Three flies. Even their pastiche was technically coordinated, and how ridiculous! I followed their gymnastics through the air, but they paid no attention to me. Were they unconsciously reproducing themselves as they flew around, with their vertiginous graphics just as we do with our convulsive twistings? I said, with a sort of rasping voice:

"Can I make you some coffee? I still have a little bit."

"No, no, my friend . . . A character that sets the tone, the vigor, a continuous point of view . . ."

"And there," Simone cut in, "I ran into Monsieur Mac's mother-in-law who told me that Monsieur Mac was at his hunting lodge, forty kilometers away. It was dark already, and I was dead tired, and to get to Monsieur Mac at that hour of the night was impossible. Fortunately a car came by . . ."

Mac O'Mac stopped in front of her—she was sitting on the bed, casually emptying her purse—and pranced. I was still in a stupor, perched on my chair rather than sitting on it, taking it all in, but not interpreting. That prancing, however, was remarkable. Continuous and irritating. One of the flies left the group and dived down, zigzagging and stopping in the air. I timidly suggested:

"Or a cup of tea? I have some tea leaves left."

The prancing moved around back of me. I said:

"You know that for me the Butts are . . ."

"I know, my friend."

Peremptory. He started to circle around me again. But my stupor had dissolved. The fly had rejoined his squadron.

"And a tone, a vigor, a continuous point of view through which the theme, the ideas, and even the style are amplified and given impetus."

And this literary technique and every turn of the crab and his noisy heels with which he enveloped me in a kind of puttee that I in turn unravelled like the wrappings of a mummy.

"I understand that," I said. "Listen. I hope for that. There surely is a way to juggle thematic material. Listen, I have already done it. I say so because I think so. But tell me this, if we agree about it, why did you come to see me? Monsieur O'Mac, I am going to start from the beginning. I am a patient man. I am not excited. Look at those flies. I gave the manuscript of *The Butts* to Simone the day before yesterday, and she took it on herself to thumb a ride on a truck to go to see you and give it to you. You say you have read it, and I take your word for it. I am asking you, right now . . ."

"Yes, my friend? But between rapt and raped there is only a difference of two letters. An intelligent critic whose name I can't remember said in 1948 that my first novel, *Holy Family,* should be inscribed . . ."

"Yes," I went on, "while I am talking, a child is dying. While we are talking, I am deteriorating, just like that wall (I pointed to it with my fingers). While we are talking, the Butts are deteriorating. Well, there is a manuscript, some scraps of paper, whether subway tickets or cigarette packages turned inside out or old wrapping paper, all held together in one corner by a neatly tied length of string, and let's call it the novel of *The Butts* . . . in the name of God! . . ."

Then I picked up the chair with both hands—I was still sitting on it—and started to turn on the same spot, staring straight at him. He stopped pacing and came over and gave me a pat on the shoulder. I don't know why, but just at that moment when I was going to pick up my chair and smash it against the wall, howling that Fabrice was dead, he said to me, almost like a father:

"Tell me, how is the boy?"

I don't know how he got there or how long he'd been there, if he came in on both feet through the door or if he had popped up out of the earth, but there was Rauss, tall and thin in those huge shoes of his (were they shrubs or privet hedges in their little green containers?), holding a bull whip in his hand, as long and thin as he, like a symbol. He closed the door, shook his fist in the air, and mashed the flies in his hand. He said:

"His boy is very sick, Monsieur. He's been in the hospital since yesterday, Mon-sieur. He had lumbar tappings yesterday. Meningitis, Mossieu! Meningitis is the inflamation of the meninx, if you please. And speaking of this, if you have any, how are your children?"

I quietly pushed back my chair and got up. He was just as surly as I. He didn't even flex his whip: a hard, cynical surliness as straight and dry and hungry as his whip.

"Who is this lout?" asked Mac.

"Rauss," I replied. "An Arabo."

"And does he usually act like a . . ."

But he suddenly noticed that no one was paying any attention to him. We were watching Simone, still sitting on the bed, slowly and methodically putting everything back into her purse. Her eyes were as hard as stone.

"The little one is very sick," said Rauss gently. "He's been in the hospital since yesterday. They gave him two lombar tappings for meningitis. And meningitis is the inflamation of the meninx. By the way, did you have a good trip, Madame?"

She closed her lipstick and put it in her purse. Her eyes were still like stone. Rauss went over to her and with an even gentler tone, almost like a supplication, repeated to her:

"The little one is very sick. He's been in the hospital since yesterday."

"Get the hell away from me!"

Suddenly she was screaming, disheveled, her cheeks burning, shaking convulsively with sobs.

"Get the hell away from me . . . Oh my God, my God, what have I done to them? Get that damned Arab out of here . . . I'm going crazy, crazy, crazy . . ."

"Now, now. Calm down," said Mac O'Mac.

"Crazy," she screamed bitterly.

"Morning, noon and night, he's always there circling like some kind of bird of bad omen. Even in my sleep, in my nightmares, there he is. In every dream and everything I do all day! I've never done anything to him, I don't say anything to him . . . He's going to drive me crazy. Do you hear me?"

"Now, now," said Mac.

He pushed Rauss to one side and helped Simone to her feet. She pulled away from him and faced Rauss. On the edges of her lips you could see foam, and I could see how she was changing—tares, avatars, education, civilization, inhibitions, fifteen centuries of European supremacy, everything was swallowed up in an instant—a good deep hatred without any fancy trimmings: flesh, guts, instincts.

"And if ever," she screamed, "if ever my child should die, do you hear me? . . . Get out! . . . Get out of here!"

"Come on now," said Mac in a strong voice.

He quickly took her out. The roar of his car reverberated like the slam of a door. I smiled. I was relaxed. I hadn't felt so relaxed in a long time.

"Who is the Christian?" Rauss asked.

He was smiling too. He smelled of animal grease. He had bent his whip into a circle, without a word, as though everything he had heard and seen had no importance at all.

"Mac O'Mac," I answered. "The author of *Holy Family.*"

"What?"

"One hundred thousand copies printed."

"Copies?"

"Yes, of his book."

He sniffed.

"Lot of stuff to burn!" he said with a sound of regret in his voice.

4

> "Later on," "will be," as in the holy scriptures. I hope that that is the way things will be some day, that it will be possible to say: "that is it" and not "it will be." People talk about the future by the ton, without restrictions . . .
>
> Vsevolod Vichnevski,
> *The Tragedy of Optimism*

I followed him into the garden.

"Or what used to be the garden," asserted Rauss. His voice sounded almost like a dog's bark, as though after trying every other possibility of human conviction (logic, the viaticum of things printed and read, the atrophy of animal *sensitivity*), he had understood that I could only accept and assimilate barking, or, at least, arguments given meaning by a tone of barking. Meanwhile he threw his head back (I was on the last step of the stairs, the overhang) and up toward the sky, into the sky, with such a sharp movement that his cap fell off. He caught it in mid-air and pulled it down over his ears with both hands, a shrivelled cap of linen as shiny as oiled paper, with a visor adorned with a faded strip of gold that had once been a naval anchor. I was surprised at my own reactions at that moment, to feel with what strength I resented all my despondency which, despite his being wholly unaware of it, was intensified by every one of his gestures and by every moment of his existence from the time he had fled from his native village in the Kabyle over that dawn-colored ocean with just two arms, two legs, thirty-two teeth, and a body with guts and head that could swallow anything, anywhere, any time.

He stood there looking at me with his eyes like narrow slits, the lids almost together, without lashes, reddened by things far removed from insomnia (he didn't even know the word); cooked, in fact, by the cement from the time he used to work as a mason. Insomnia was something familiar to me, something I was familiar with that had turned my eyelids purple and as thin as cigarette paper. There was a kind of exasperation in the shortness of his breathing, something both calm and expectant.

"Because this used to be a garden," he howled. "Look at those trees, or what's left of them. Because they never belonged to you. That's why you passed judgement on them. You came here one morning, with two good arms, two legs, and they were your weapons for the sacking. And two good eyes to supervise your masterwork, and to give approval. Once there were thirty-seven of them. Now there are only two. So well adjudged that they pose the equation (not even that: trees equal heat, there was that also) but: this elusive and exasperating knowledge that, whatever you may have done in the past or do in the future, not a single fallen leaf belongs to you or ever will belong to you. That and nothing else. They had been fruit trees. I can still remember their names, like designations of strange birds cited in some dead language: trees of plums, cherries, apples, pears . . . Cut at the base as though by strokes of hatred, they stood there now like statue bases that dirty Arab Rodin the Second could be set up on, or play poker with your own shadow, betting your destiny or your failure that you shower with affection and nourish like a virus. Symbol, prism, explained an old dictionary that I thumbed through last week like a teller going through a stack of bills (an illusion I still cherish) before I sold it to the ragpicker. Creation through the medium of Yalaan Waldik: I am here to applaud you. The two trees left aren't really trees anymore. They know their future is irrevocable. They look like two gray gestures in a gray sky—stretching upward toward that nonsense of a sky, two arms, threatening and full of terror."

We dropped wearily onto the curb of a well. I remember it as a kind of surrender. For whole days and nights I had been lucid and relaxed. On the other side of the little wall of birch trees, spongy with humidity, with all of the felinity of a cat and the awkwardness of a goose, I saw Josepha in her yard slithering from tree to tree. Furtive, a crone so old that the skin of her face, between two leaps, looked even whiter than her hair. She leaned against a tree trunk and pushed her glasses up on her forehead. *Poor Simone!* I could almost hear her think, I knew her so well and hated her so much. *The Arabo's out of prison, poor Simone! We'd better keep an eye on things over there.*

At the same time, Rauss saw her. Or, to be more accurate, caught a glimpse of her. She stood up and sat back down, so quickly you could hardly tell one movement from the other. I admit I wondered if anything had happened, if he had seen anything of her at all. Maybe she hadn't really appeared, never existed except as a corollary to my own drama, like a simple spot of ink between two retorts. Because she had disappeared even before Rauss got up, as if a trap had opened up at her feet.

But the fact was inescapable, more pitiless than memory, more implacable than any judgement, any hatred or any pardon, and I think: *She is just stooping. With that simultaneity and that quickness of decision and action that charitable souls have who are devoted to the wellbeing of their fellowmen: one of those kewpie dolls at the fair that you knock over with a rubber ball.*

Rauss was looking at me now. Attentively, hardly breathing, trying to understand. It was as though I were a mirror in which he could see himself, could analyse and recognize himself to the point of identification and of doubt. Then he started to speak, haltingly, densely, and almost without expression:

"No," he said, "I will never understand. For your concubine to jump on me like a mad dog, I can understand. What she was doing was attacking you. Nothing more natural than to get mixed up in your private hatreds and your family avatars, and the fate they call meningitis that your kid's got. You're an Arabo and so am I. Same bag, same contents, so much alike that even Simone wouldn't know the difference if I took your place in bed some night. Hey! You smell like me, and I'll smell like you. Same odor, one and the same, the smell of failure. Even I admit to that. You heard her a while ago, didn't you? She said: if ever, if ever my child dies. And I was already bending my back for future stonings. I admit that. What I can't admit, what gets me confused, is this: when, how, and in what dark destiny of God could I ever have loved you?"

And I thought: doubt may come some day. Like the cat. I couldn't understand why that animal loved me. He had grabbed me by the wrists and held them in his hand. Yes, doubt will come to him one day, and he'll be like me. Maybe he already has some doubts. Maybe I'll have the same fate the cat had. And soon.

That day it was like getting a load off my back. Unloading my present, my past and my future, as well as our lay blood, a few civilizations' blood removed from what made Arab steeds and Arab conquerors gallop on in that time of hegira of sand, of thirst and of faith, and with every gallop, the credo: "Thou shalt live, not by the rhythm, but with the intensity of the galloping . . ." Yes, not very far distant: several centuries' wisps of straw in the maw of time, several wars that made merchants out of us, several stains on honor and dignity, but the race is still there with its nose forever Semitic, still living with the rhythm of the earth—just as our blood ever since then had traced it in our veins: "That man there," my blood said, "is one you will love. Without ever asking why. Completely, without an iota of intelligence or of hope. With the fanaticism of religion." I have doubts, my brother.

He let my wrists go and took me by the neck. That was the way it was: always knowing, always the critical sense and the intelligence that tortured, the soul that came to us from the Occident, the germ of alienation and degeneration: because at that very moment, I was nothing more than an open wound. An all-powerful lucidity, as keen as a razor, took hold of me (and I would even qualify it as necessary, redemptive, the verdict of this language of love so unworthy of me, as intelligence cried out: "Your hatreds are so ancient, so functional" and I recognized it and gloried in it), the lucidity to ask myself how Josepha, still stooping somewhere (all-seeing and all-hearing) was going to interpret our two faces so close they were almost touching.

"Yes," Rauss whispered, "Simone has doubts too. The Butts also. And the cat you killed had doubts. And the trees you cut down. So does this garden, broken up, turned upside down, piled up with garbage. And these charred doors. And even your soul—people are afraid of anybody that talks about a soul, but I'm talking about it because with the least look of defiance, I'll beat the hell out of you. Yes, every one of those creatures left something inside you. Simone, her house and her flesh, her human evolution and perhaps her love, or to be more exact, the eventuality of loving you. She never ceased being ready, and no doubt it's still not too late. She probably doesn't know that herself. She says she hates me: because she knows that I know what she does not. And me, as though I'd slipped inside your skin like a mollusk in a new shell. And the Butts! Don't forget that they did not name you their guide or chief or spokesman or any identifiable official whatsoever: that's how the corporal serves them; they made you their soul. Even the idea of hope, of a social and human solution to their miseries, of a destiny finally man's destiny, it's you yourself (talking, gesturing, saying such words as liberty, happiness, ideal, right to their face as you would throw a coin to a beggar), you yourself who forged it and sealed it in them. It's the only thing that makes a man live or die. The only thing that can't be manipulated, like the Word of God or nitroglycerine, neither by prophet nor by expert. So deeply encrusted in them, a quintessence, cellular, that from the very moment on they have lived only in a state of projection into the future. They have ceased to live since then. Not only did it go in through their ears never to come out again, it became their soul. Before that, they had lost their soul. They were the Butts. Among the 300,000 Arabs in France, they were the residue, the outcasts. They never had the choice between the two attitudes with which to confront the world: change for the better or defiance. No, even that choice was not theirs to make: they left their soul on the other side of the Mediterranean. They weren't even aware of it. They were perfectly happy with their viscera. But one day, you came along and told them: you will be men, you will be happy, and you will be free. Prophet of a pigmy's stature, you should know that that night they killed. Killed as a group, deliberately, like a single man, with a single knife, at the same fraction of a second. Killed because they began to see that the soul you had given them, unsatisfied, unused, made them suffer too much."

Yes, the sky was still there. It always had been there, but if it hadn't existed, man would have invented it. Immutably present above our heads—and the blind have seen it and the deaf have heard it and the paralytic dances on it—our symbol of symbols, the boomerang of our instincts and the target of our weaknesses. Yes, weighing this September morning with its thick clouds, gray, wet and heavy, charged with electricity and thunder, with expectation and patience, as if they were held in place there only by some laughable dabs of flour paste.

The symbol was right in the mouth of the Arabo. It was not quite closed, still forming the final syllable. And I quietly thought: *Never. Doubt will never become a reality: it will remain doubt. He does not doubt me. He doubts himself. They all have doubts about themselves. It is not hope that I have taught them, but doubt.* And what I mean by that is not a simple reprimand, but the desperate and undisguised expression of their doubt. I said: " 'We will get inside these Arabs like a knife cutting into butter,' Marshall Saint-Arnaud once declared."

Then I realized that I had just cited something from a work on political science—if not from some dime novel—and that I had done so with the proper gravity of tone, neither convincingly nor convinced, simply erudite. Blowing from the clouds, the wind had exactly the grating sound of rusty hinges. Weighted down with the moistness of those clouds, with the same grayness, with the same current, with the same patience, as though it were the very voice of the heavens.

"Who is that?" asked Rauss.

"Arnaud," I explained staidly. "Armand-Jacques Leroy de Saint-Arnaud, Marshall of France, born in Paris and died at sea, 1801–1854."

Rauss stayed seated. Not a hair of his head moved, despite the violent and strident wind—on the contrary, his hair took on the plastered look of cement.

"Don't know 'im," he finally said. It wasn't just sincerity, the cynical and brutal expression of a cynical and brutal sincerity. It was something entirely different: that credibility that was special to

Rauss, to North Africans and to Polish miners, with their limits well defined by the very borders of sensitivity and beyond which words have no real meaning.

"I don't know him," repeated Rauss. This time he very carefully separated the syllables like so many nails, as if the amalgam were a gangue; as if by detaching them he were probing the last meanderings of his memory at the same time. "I don't think I know him. Even if he were still alive, I don't need any references. What's more, I don't know any marshalls. And even more, I don't know how or why any Frenchman, even a marshall, would come between life and me."

He was pensive for a moment. He had let go of my wrists and wasn't looking at anything, not even at the sky. The wind was howling, raucous, violent, and moving fast.

"Don't even know you," he added. "I know. You think you can take things back to their beginning and live like a kind of transplant, a refuge from all impotence, an escape from all mediocrity. I understand very well. But if you go back to the matter of Marshall Saint-Arnaud? Go on with your intellectual stuff. I keep my projects on a level I can understand: I want enough to eat to keep alive tomorrow."

Seated at my window—closed, but even closed the wind comes through it as though it were gauze—I am patience itself. I have taken refuge in patience, and that's all I have left. Night suddenly fallen, and the wind is black and even freer and more savage.

I hear it grating like two rows of teeth, non-stop, without a pause—until the moment I realize it is my own teeth that are grinding. And even then, it is nothing more than a dead leaf shining in the wind.

I don't ask anyone to understand me. I sowed the seeds and I have harvested bristles. Rauss said as much over a period of three hours, uninterrupted, hammering like a blacksmith on an anvil, a blacksmith with no eyes, no ears, no guts, animated by the need to hammer—and counting a steady rhythm to his strokes. Three hours. So stubborn in loving me that I finally got to my feet with a gleam of murder in my eyes.

At the same time, I said to myself, Josepha also must have stood up. Neither Rauss nor I looked at her. With white hair, white skin, white bones and flesh, so far gone beyond old age and what used to be a human being that the savage wind must have swept her away, freeing her in a handful of white powder, the basic salt of respectability of pious souls. I wish them all reunion with the imponderable dust of time. But no one saw her get up. We were both there, I standing in the wind, Rauss still sitting on the edge of the well. And I said to myself that, even transcribed into terms of calculus, with the constant H for reforming the motion of determinism and the constant C for the revision of the concepts of space and time, the absurdity of man would never be resolved. What I was thinking was: *I'll never live except in the absurd. For ten years now my brain, my Arab brain thinking in Arabic, has been grinding away at European concepts, in such an absurd way it transforms them into gall and even the brain gets sick from it. And if it goes on thinking, it is not by theorem of adaptation but because through all of its pulverizing, it is overwhelmed with proliferating membranes—the only part that has adapted to the occidental world.*

He walked off into the black wind. As I sit here now at my window, I understand what he was saying as he ambled down the cement walk, adjusting his cap with little taps of his fist and thread-thin in his blue mechanic's overalls. Or more like the pounding of his shoes that I can still hear like distant echoes. Not a moment, he said, not a single moment of rest . . . I won't let you have a single moment of rest . . .

The sound of his footsteps stopped. The night and the wind are black. Behind the window, crouching like a buzzard, I inhale them—partners in the single breath that fills my lungs to capacity. I don't want to think. I am all patience. My teeth grate and the wind rasps. I know now that there is nothing but my own voice, strident and savage and full of infinite patience.

5

"No. I'm not hungry, thank you. But you eat."

The words, weighty in their consistancy and their color, were spoken like so many gray pebbles ejected by a sudden triggering of the tongue. Her eyes were shifty, restless, not frightened, but full of despair: as though she were in back of them and were trying to make them stop moving in their orbits. The wind had been quiet for some time, and it surprised me.

Upright in the fireplace—I had stuffed it in that way by sheer force—the chair was slowly dissolving.

"After a while," I said. "How is Fabrice?"

She sighed, then took off her skirt and her shoes, then slipped between the covers: "Condition unchanged. We'll see tomorrow."

She pressed the light switch. I was crouched in front of the fire. Crackling, hissing, tongues of ochre and burnt sienna flame. Along with me, as the heat began to rouse them, a whole tumult of smells crouched too: old clothing, bitter flesh, a poor man's breath.

"Do you think Mac will do something for me?"

"No doubt about it. He was very positive about your manuscript. He may even write a preface for it himself."

"Did he say he would?"

"Not exactly, but he implied it."

"When?"

"Well . . . a little while ago. In the restaurant."

She quickly went on (I could hardly see her in the darkness, but I knew she was stiffening like a hunting dog on quarry, and the thought came to me: *now her eyes are fully immobile, straight-forward and clear*):

"I went with him to a Chinese restaurant in the Latin Quarter. He insisted that I eat something. I had a sandwich."

The chair was completely consumed by now. Rauss would have said that the Hegira had changed nothing, neither decadence nor European supremacy nor symbiosis, that in the matter of seating, excepting on an ass, the horse, the camel or a straw mat—all, like him, products of the earth—the Arab has never been able to sit anywhere except on earth. In his concept, a chair, that product of civilization that smiles at the sweat of a man, represents nothing more than a log or a faggot. I heard the chair burn up as if it had whispered a secret, but I had made no mistake: it was the ultimate offense. And I began to fantasize, in the fireplace that was consuming me in my turn along with the smoking remains of that chair now just an ember, as one lights a cigarette from the butt of another: I could have whispered my regret at having lived.

"Simone . . ."

"Yes?"

Perhaps in fear. Perhaps in cowardice. I was like that for years. Fearful and cowardly.

"Are you asleep?"

"No."

I stirred some little pieces of wood in the embers and blew on them. Several sparks rekindled, shabby and ashamed. They could have sprung to life—these bits of wood might have been spared—or have been no more than sparks. I too felt shabby and ashamed.

"Don't you think I have changed?"

There was a crackle. Even a piece of wood has the right to an explosion, to a death rattle, to its final sign of life. But even if the whole creation of the Western World were to be consumed, I would say: "My forebears were Arabs, and I have lived as an Arab. I found them deeply committed, not to a belief or a destiny, but to their immemorial misery, and I will follow their path to the end: misery certainly must lead to something."

"No."

I said to myself: even a chair or a cat. One, perhaps tomorrow, ashes, will be at the end of the garden. The other one is already there underneath a heavy stone and three shovelfuls of earth. The chair did nothing to me, nor did the cat. I was not born sadistic. I don't know even now if I am or if I ever have been. But if gestures or tracings of acts, or stammerings, can be translated into statistical values in the eyes of society, then I may be called sadistic—and I am proud of it.

"I've just spent six months in prison. You don't find anything changed about me?"

"No, not really."

"Am I keeping you from sleeping?"

"Not at all."

I got up and walked toward the bed. My smells went with me. I would have liked the hand I placed on her forehead to be as soft as down.

"You know Simone . . ."

"Yes? . . ."

I had surely reduced her to the level of human residue as well. The intention was certainly praiseworthy, the source in the emotions, the capacity to love. In my hands, tools have shattered like delicate antiques. Or rather, accustomed to working without tools, I have accorded them much more importance than the work to be done: systems, police, unions . . . everything that transforms the individual into mass-man: it was precisely from that problem that the Butts suffered. It was not their lack of capacity to adapt, but the tenacious insistence that was deployed in making them adapt. Lack of experience (postulate, goal—and the cementing between the two confines: a man's life) was all that saved them.

One day I found myself in her path—the straight path of respectability and of stability. If I did not find myself there, it was because I had lost my way. I had lured her into a dead-end street for Arabos, with an entrance but no exit. Arabos have a proclivity for such blind alleys. Like them, they too are stunted, burrows in the ground, drab day and night. They come out of their hole only by night, but they don't go very far . . . Daylight wounds them, dignity lies in wait for them, and they slink along walls dressed in their coats as drab as themselves and their burrows. That's why they run back into their holes, wounded small animals who are ashamed to die in broad daylight.

"Simone, will you forgive me?"

"What for?"

I caressed her forehead and then her cheek. Even though my

hand was only flesh and bone. And I said to myself that perhaps this hand had touched that forehead and cheek so that it would stop its caressing. But I also said to myself: you're afraid, you're a coward. I said to myself: the chair and the cat. I soaked up suffering and hatred. They were both familiar to me, so much a part of my psychological makeup that I am suspicious of any pleasure.

"What for, for God's sake?"

"What do I know? You deserve something better, a quiet, uncompromising life. I've been your damnation."

"Don't blame yourself for it."

"Yes, I've been your damnation."

I began to stroke her neck. Maybe it was at that instant that I thought of the cat, and she must have felt it too. Under my fingers, the neck suddenly stiffened. I struck a light, and she was brutally exposed. She was too surprised to cry out.

"What's going on?"

Her arms stiffened against her sides, and the hundred watts of the lightbulb glaringly revealed how tense she was, like a reaction to something repulsive or intensely disgusting. Only her legs were trembling, almost imperceptibly, but that too added to the physical stiffness. Her jawbones were jutting out, and her eyes were set—no corneas, no expression, no sign of pupils; the reaction to the need, first and foremost, to control the eyes and keep them from trembling and giving away her feelings, as if the rest of her body might shamelessly betray the inner being.

"What's going on?" I repeated.

I bent over her, smelling her body. I covered her and turned out the light. She smelled of fear.

"I came back from prison yesterday morning," I said. (I could hear the sound of my own voice: little particles of sound, gathered up and compressed into a sediment, devoid of emotion, of expression, and even of meaning. I was thinking: *just as one weighs a bowling ball, weighing not the weight or the distance of the trajectory or even all of that at one and the same time, but time itself; the instant of the present that one tries to immobilize intensely as if to find a refuge.*)

"You were waiting for me at the garden gate, because you could not do anything else but wait for me."

Yes: she could do nothing else but wait for me. After all, Rauss had come to the prison gate to wait for me! "See you later!" He had pumped my hand and in a couple of bounds had been on his way. I understood that: fear of words, that reserve that shied away from verbal expression. Stealing a chunk of meat was his way of welcoming me back.

"I had the manuscript of *The Butts* under my arm. I had written it in prison and I held it out for you as a gift and a promise that I made to you a long time ago. You insisted on leaving right away to take what I had written to Mac, whom you did not know. I only saw him this morning for the first time, and we talked amicably. More accurately, I used to write him when I had the price of a stamp, but he never answered me . . . No, don't say anything. Just breathe quietly. I don't quite know myself why I'm talking so much."

As I leaned over her, I had the sensation of seeing a pair of shears. A kind of fear of cutting something, dizziness, a drama that was anesthetizing her. But she was struggling against it. The covers were barely enough to shield her; I knew how desperately she was trying to be calm, and that the more she tried, the stiffer she became. A leaf fell somewhere in the garden, for I heard it fall.

"Fabrice must have grown a lot. Must have been waiting for me too: he was sick. Not a child's sickness, not leprosy or typhoid or the plague, those illnesses that Arabs or Arab customs were used to, no, it was meningitis. That's a barbaric notion, abstract, indigestible, of the same family as atheism, politics, or cancer. Inflammation of the meninges, Rauss called it. I don't even know what that is. A club that had hit me on the head, I strangled the cat. He had epileptic fits. He must have contaminated my son, I'll bet you on it. Even if he'd been fat and healthy, I would have strangled him. After all, I spent six months in prison because of you, so don't forget: that dumb peasant that called you an Arabo's woman got his in a good beating. Don't forget it. You know what that means for me: one more conviction and I'm deported. What did Mac say to you?"

I heard her try to open her mouth, to pull her tongue away from the palate. My forehead was covered with perspiration.

"In a minute," I said to her. "Right now, just try to breathe quietly."

Suddenly she let out a terrifying scream.

I turned on the light and then turned it off. A drop of sweat had just fallen on her face, a drop of molten sweat.

"Just a drop of sweat," I explained to her. "Come on now. Calm down!"

Outside was the night and the wind. One blowing in the other, bringing it life, electrifying it. There must have been stars high up in the sky, like sparks of laughter. And from the horizon upwards and from there back to earth and at the cardinal points, the *widening* of night's vastness. As though the earth had waited until the sun had died (the light of the sun that so pitilessly limits man: his horizon, his dwellings, his frontiers, his gateways, his desires, his needs, his flags, his gods, his fellow men) and let the lights, voices, and men's presences be drowned in a fundamental blackness so that another life beyond all human limitations will emerge.

A last spiral of flame flared up in the fireplace.

"Simone," I said, disillusioned, "I don't know what I am going to do. It isn't the prison. There you are, as stiff as a board, and I'm sick of it. For God's sake, let me go to sleep. I'm exhausted . . . I'm talking like a wreck, leaning over you like a desolation. Coming out of prison was life, Simone. The beginning of life. For me and for you. But to carry something inside yourself, deeply, intensely, for a very long time, like an ulcer—and to act always thinking of that ulcer, not man, not beast, from one prison to another, ashamed, belittled, beaten, but with the conviction that as long as you carry that something inside, nothing can happen to you, nothing can vilify you in your own eyes, just as Christ carried his cross, the conviction that words signify nothing, change nothing, neither systems nor hovels nor gifts of money or of nature; the conviction that I, the element in that checkered mosaic that Press Agencies call North Africans, that my responsibility was not to redeem myself vis-à-vis the society I am living in because I have a claim to its sympathy, *but that I must redeem North Africans.* Suffer for them in my dignity as a man and in my flesh as a man. That is what I have been doing for five years. Then translate that into a sort of testimony, not of my senses, but of my sufferings. After that was done, I had to adjust to myself and to the society in which I had to live. I had to unearth the individual who had been forgotten for five years. It was not complicated. Do you remember? When I met you four years ago, my first words were about the Arabos. Those 300,000 North Africans. And I, speaking and writing in French, trying to transmit their misery and their distress. If you count sixty kilos per Arab, you end up with some 20,000 tons of suffering. That day I saw your eyes, Simone. They were human. Neither beautiful nor enthusiastic. Not even a woman's eyes. Simply human, and I thought I saw in them, as Antony did in Cleopatra's, a whole flight of galleys. I said to myself: if only a single pair of European eyes would agree to *see* my 300,000 Arabos, their miseries would disappear. Now, Simone, if I tell you that I don't know what I'm going to do or even what I am, you must believe me. Just as you must believe this: something has happened, something I'm trying to grasp. Once I do, I'll go all the way. You know me well enough to know that this is neither a threat nor an affirmation. It is a simple fact."

I turned the light on and then off again. Her eyes had aged four years.

"I told Rauss to leave. He flexed his riding whip fiercely. Even to be chased away like that was part of his fulfillment. An Arabo is always ready to move on, resignedly. Resignation for him is forgetfulness, privation. He has so much of resignation that it's become a kind of marketplace for scrap-iron. Maybe he was waiting for me to use that German term to get out: Raus! He walked away with a brief laugh, as sardonic and brief as the neighing of a mare. That meant that there was nothing left of the Arab in me, that I was nothing more than a slavey of the Boches, nothing but a distant cousin of those gutteral orders of the Nazi work brigades in TODT. He had his first schooling in it, and lost his real name. Raus! Get a move on! Get out! That's his name now. A simple negation, a simple ejection."

"Let me go to sleep!"

"I watched while you were screaming. I didn't know you were a racist. When I was talking to you about Fabrice, what weariness were you screaming? I was watching you scream. I didn't know you were so worn out. And for that exhaustion, wasn't Mac responsible?"

"Please, please let me go to sleep!"

I turned on the light and turned it off again. I heard a husky voice that sounded like the scratching of chalk on a blackboard.

"Sleep! And I should get to sleep too, shouldn't I? That's all there is left to do, get some sleep. Tomorrow we'll wake up. What for, in God's name? What you want is for me to wake up mute and you deaf, permanently! There's one thing, Simone. Even if I had to bellow in the ears of a cadaver, I wouldn't go to bed until I knew what happened. Do you hear me?"

I turned the light on and turned it off again. Since I had to know! Far beyond the senses, instinctive, animal and innate, consciousness persists. Those senses that we have made as omniscient and as generative as mathematical axioms through which man enters life and leaves it, *lives* this life (and if he misses one of the formulas, he is tagged as *unfit)* like the ball and chain of a galley slave or a truncheon blow. It makes the brain the dominating center to the detriment of all of man's being (and he himself, among all the other faculties making conscious intelligence predominate; a Judas in the face of infinity, but the rest is well closed off, well barricaded, the triumph of the idea of property and the triumph of Europe); senses, whether black or canine, have adapted to Europe, so that even to us Arabs those rations (a viaticum) of liberty, equality and fraternity might be allocated. But consciousness lives on, and no prison ever taught me or succeeded in smothering it in me, no misery, no civilization: it was an open wound! Consciousness that a while ago with Rauss had *formed* me: the rejection of the Butts and of all their problems: *the wholly intuitive iota that something had gone on while I was in prison, and the determination to get to the core of it no matter what.*

"Mac O'Mac." I stressed that, and she gasped for breath. At the same time, I clapped my hands together as if to kill a fly. "Mac O'Mac," I repeated. "Him and nobody else. No doubt you were hatching something. It was more like a feeling than knowing it, like a bizarre odor, painful, at most irritating—and at most, I admit it, with this item: sooner or later I would wash all that from top to bottom by the bucketful. But the part that the incubation finally hatched ends up in a single name: Mac O'Mac."

I knew I was right. I didn't even need to say it, to translate it or even to think it. She didn't either. We were a couple of donkeys properly beaten, and who could do nothing but bray. Yes, the need to explain what must have happened was like the braying of an ass—the justification of our omnipotent lucidity. Yes, Simone, my poor child, but you're wasting your time with that Arab, wasting your youth and even your resources.

"Let me go to sleep!"

Yes, the virtual and the real have a common measurement, with neither frontiers nor limits beyond human understanding. Now I was fully aware of my intuitions. It was as if I had enlarged the dimensions of my being, as if I had exploded myself.

I knew by the inflections of voice, the nominal value of words and of pauses, so unconsidered that I thought: *Mac may not have said any of those things. He may not even have thought them.* But I could hear him: he doesn't even have a job, he said. He confuses what he wants with reality. I've reread his letters several times. He's the typical example of an intellectual, or rather of a pseudo-intellectual from another continent, from another compendium of history. He handles our language fairly well and our European pettifoggeries, but that's as far as it goes. Our history, the efforts of two millenia of Frenchmen, accumulated drop by drop, idea by idea, life by life, and our institutions that have grown one out of the other, all of that is foreign to him. He is not the end product, as we both are. Even in the problem of the North Africans which is so close to his heart, he is absolutely not with it. He forgets that he wanted to address a French audience with French reactions, and that he anticipates nothing beyond the printed page. It's precisely in the area of his private life that he has been wrong as far as you are concerned. Not only does he not comport himself as a pseudo-European, not only does he destroy our concepts of the standard Arabo, he even goes so far as to forget that all we ask of him is to be purely and simply an Arabo. But he has the pretension, the ambition, and the naiveté to want (his writing makes it very clear) to impose the Orient on Europe. The results were inevitable. Just think about it, I ask you: daughter-mother, no job, no stability, no money, no family, no future, nothing but the street or suicide or daily degradation. If I understand correctly . . .

"I WANT TO GO TO SLEEP!"

I turned on the lamp and turned it off again. She didn't want to go to sleep at all. Or to be precise, she had already been asleep. Now she was waking up and speaking in a loud voice in the dark, like a frightened child, as though to assure herself that nothing had happened and she could go back to sleep.

"If I understand things, the house in Villejuif belongs to you. When you met your lover, he was just out of prison, and he used up all your savings. He gave you promises in exchange. And a gritting of teeth, as bitter as the cat's meowing. And great resolutions that, according to him, are capable of attaining the stars. But, my dear, our mission is to civilize, and I cannot allow an Arab to barbarize a representative of the French people . . ."

"I beg of you, Yalaan, I beg of you . . ."

I turned on the light and turned it off again. She was still sleeping, she had not stopped sleeping.

"That's what he must have said to you. It was like the sound of a clock striking, capable of bringing other sounds of clocks striking out of the past. It's true I've been stupid not to hear them, far away and tempting. Cain, what have you done with your brother? I'm twenty-two years old, after all; I am a house owner, I'm still attractive, there's no shortage of young workers who take life seriously, I'd have an unexciting life, but it would be quiet and stable, I could satisfy my hunger, sleep as long as I want, stop thinking and torturing myself.

Those problems of Arabs bore the hell out of me."

I did not turn out the light. I might as well have. Nothing made any sense any more, not even things done instinctively, without conscious thought. Somewhere deep inside of me, beyond this drama, beyond the world of my anxieties, of masochism and derision—and which must have been as insignificant to her as a water bubble—behind that window to which I turned my back when my impulse was to go up to it and fuse myself with it: wooden fittings, panes, bolts, nails, putty, paint. I could hear the laughter of the wind in the darkness of the night.

"I'd still be here, Simone. An Arab. Even intellectual. You don't feed an Arab, even if he is an intellectual, with words of love, concepts of love, of a home and family, with expressions he has never heard before, words that no one knows in the mountains of Algeria and that my co-religionists would take for the voice of machine tools or the whirring of birds' wings. So European that this poor dumbbell of an Arab would only understand them four years later: hmm; you won't do . . . you don't have a diploma . . . I thought . . . so what can be done about it? . . . after all, it's not my fault . . ."

I turned the light on. But I already knew. I had already known it before the first time I saw her woman's eyes. Now, curiously enough, they were drawn back, empty, even non-existent, two black slits. Failure underscored twice by a black pencil. I turned out the light.

Black was the night outside. I knew that the night was not even patient: the receptacle at best for this wind that thought that it could impose its law on her, its violence, and that night would calmly devour it.

I turned on the light and left it on.

"There would still be our son: without my name, I have no legal right to him—and I've never bought anything for him, not even a bottle of milk. That means that I have no human right to him either. Take a father's love, wrap it up in a newspaper and toss it in the garbage! Like refuse, amen!"

I got undressed and lay down beside Simone. Then I turned off the light. I knew what I was doing. There were far more persuasive arguments than words, or sentiments expressed in the form of words. And that's the way it was: I burst out in anger, and she smelled of fear. It was with such odors (more like sweating than odors—but she was sweating anger and it was I who was sweating fear) that we embraced each other.

I turned on the light, ground out some words, and turned out the light.

That went on until dawn.

I turned the light on. Above my head, the lamp burned its tube, yellow, set, sardonic, like the eyes of a cyclops.

Turned off, there above my head, it patiently waited for me to turn it on again, even more sardonic.

Somewhere, somewhere in the room (no doubt the wind had started up again), there was the sound of a flight of bees. It must have been my voice.

Dawn was tinting the windowpanes. What dawn? Human idiocy has no dawn, nor self-depreciation nor pompous nonsense: no dawn! It had tinted the windowpanes, tinted the leaden eyes of Simone, tinted the shadow of my body against the wall, half-sitting on the bed, half naked, caught between fatigue and fury—a bleeding dawn against the window, turning her closed lids purple. My shadow was as green as a mouthful of bile.

That went on for four days and four nights.

Wear and tear, I learned in the dictionary, is the deterioration brought about by use and by rubbing. But even then I knew that wear and tear was something else again: it was degradation.

She got up very early, made the bed, sat on it for hours on end, with her back straightened and her eyes set—facing the window, silica and wood like her—the sun either came out or did not come out, clouds passed either high or low in the sky, and now and then, as though from nowhere, hardly perceptible, already extinct and dead, and with a hyena's leap, came the wind. It was like a cannon shot that clutched the earth and shook it, as one might shake an enormous rug, then suddenly leaving it curiously quiet and serene. Simone was perceptively more and more hardened, more and more harsh.

Now and then a foot would kick open the door, and a hand would toss in a slice of liver or a portion of rice (stolen, cold, but already cooked) on the floor. I said to myself: *it must be Rauss.* Aloud, I said:

"Eat something."

"No, thank you. I'm not hungry. Eat something yourself," she would say.

The door had been closed for quite a while. I said to myself: *It must be Rauss. It's all a part of his brusque love, that I want no part of, exactly the way this woman wants no part of mine, with one important difference. I accept it like a coward.* I had not even heard his galoshes on the walk. I had not heard him coming.

"You're not hungry?"

"No."

I pushed her cheeks with my thumb and index finger, exactly at the jawbone, until she opened her mouth. Then I stuffed in some little scraps of food. She swallowed, almost without chewing. Then I made her drink a glass of water. All by force.

She could have walked out, but she didn't. With one bound, she could have been free and put kilometers, atmospheres, and the people between herself and this dangerous tension. Protection For The Girl, yes my dear do sit down and calm yourself just where is this Arab? We must call the Police right away—yes, she could have done that, but she stayed where she was.

I could have counted her eyelashes, they were that still and dry; she went from one corner of the room to another, not because she needed movement either as counter-irritant or even to break the monotony. It was because the corner of the bed or the piece of floor where she had been sitting finally was boring, she would cross her arms, wring her hands, knot her fingers; they were gestures without even the value of gestures, a cause, a symbol, dressed in a pleated skirt and a sweater that she took off at night as though she had done nothing: they waited for her, hanging on a peg, keeping their own form, supple and empty. When she put them back on when night was over, they were not even damp or softened, still tepid with the exact warmth of the night before. My God, I know something is going to happen to me . . .

Two or three times, from somewhere, I heard someone call a name: Simone! It was like sound coming through water. Amplified, moist with curiosity, and no doubt, with Christian concern. But they were Christian voices, nothing more. And I thought: *or the wind. The humming of the wind. It has become Christian too.* I went over to the window, but I did not open it. The calm thin face behind the pane, ready to break it, ready to smash it into bits, and I gauged it. There was a group of old women and men gathered behind the privet hedge. Their fists shook frenetically in the air. Slowly I turned my back on them. The wind blew dead leaves against the shrubbery.

The fourth dawn came.

Neither bleeding nor yellow nor green. A simple grayish trail across a gray horizon.

She jumped out of bed and screamed: "This can't go on!"

I saw only her eyes: they were only lids. Granular, saffron-yellow, slightly bleary, and slit by a black line: like the half-closed lids of the cadavers of birds.

"This can't go on," I admitted. "What are we going to do?"

She crossed her arms. The dawn took hold of her, and she shivered.

"You know what you have to do."

"Meaning what?"

She walked over to the door and opened it to the wind.

6

Perhaps it is dawn at the edge of a forest, a mist rising from the earth, the melodious awakening of birds, and the discreet murmuring of trees. Perhaps also in the Kabyle in Algeria, there is a thin and timid sun, soon to be the sovereign of all space, between two equinoctial storms. Or simply compressed, restrained, almost distilled light—royal blue or soft rose—coming through a distant lampshade.

He is sitting there—and I recognize him. Only his tail end is seated on the very edge of the chair. Mac probably told him to sit down three or four days ago. But he hears the voice, the inflections of the voice and its resonances only now. In perhaps another three or four days he will understand the words themselves, the value of each one of them, and the meaning of the whole sentence:

"Sit down . . . I'll be with you right away . . . What hell it is to be famous and to have a telephone . . ."

Those people who saw him go by did not say anything, did not stop, no doubt did not even see him. If there had been some quiet remarks from a charitable soul or some touch of a helping hand, no echo of it resounded in his conscience. His conscience had been extinguished for quite a while, as though a blind man's dog (a blind man who was deaf, dumb, and debrained) had perhaps led him into Mac O'Mac's office and indicated with a pointing foot where to sit, then left him there.

There are two black shoes side by side on the carpet. They explain nothing, but they exhale distress. He can move his toes timidly and clumsily. But he still does not know that these shoes are his and that feet fit into them. A voice in the room whispers or breaks out in Indian cries or an Arab poem. He is tired. He vaguely feels that his bones are only the breaking of bones, as though someone had just hit him with a piece of lead.

The pain is completely physical. He is accustomed to physical pain and does not notice it, but beyond pain is that unhealthy torpor that he does not like. His sweat glands have been at work and go on producing a kind of grayish, brackish, thick oil, that anoints him like a toad's skin. Even his hair, his clothes, his shoes, and even his senses, are impregnated with it. His voice fell silent too—and now there is a silence there that is unhealthy too—thick and oily.

Why, why in God's name, one day in his youth had he polished the shoes of that Catholic from Bône? He looks down at his feet, there on the carpeting before him, and he can take pride in them: all of Europe (the mirage of the North) in miniature there in that pair of shoes that he can calmly polish all the rest of his life.

Meanwhile the angry voice starts up again, and Mac O'Mac's hand shakes him. Before the eyes full of perspiration, of tears and of mist, there hangs a face: perhaps Mac's, or perhaps the numberless faces of Europe seen through his distress, a series of masks cut out of cardboard, colorful and vengeful, one dizzily substituting for another: Descartes, Kant, Bergson, William James, the masks of bridges and of pylons, of pioneers and of men who cut rivers into quarters, ratiocinations and powers, missionaries of materialism and of the machine gun, those who solicit and those who lay claim, specialists in everything from zero to human dignity, and later on those who discovered that all discoveries still have to be rediscovered, all because they had been found through the "Know Thyself" of Aristotle that seemed to be an invitation to explore the ego and as such made a fool of the whole Occident—while its frenetic and desparate search for reality lured it on, not wanting to awaken in its being what is carefully called the conscience—other labyrinths of his soul, choked shut since his childhood, that suddenly were illuminated. It was as if what Mac was yelling at him, right into his face, was the language of a robot, or what he could no longer understand as being French.

Yes, here I sit. I am even pitiable enough to act the sybarite and to wedge myself comfortably into this chair which, he reminds me, is one of the finest and best of the Empire chairs with arms in the form of swan's necks. And then, there are my shoes, and those cartileges covered with flesh that are designated auricular chambers with which

I hear what Mac has to say.

". . . Yes, my friend," he said to me, "she telephoned. You were destined to be only a passing fancy, with no future in her life. No, it couldn't go on. Sooner or later you would have killed her. She took the bull by the horns, since it is her own home . . ."

But I don't understand. I don't want to know who or what he's talking about. At the most, by the inner comprehension that I discover and that soothes me and stops the secretions of my glands, I have the sensation of an ancient and very deep suffering which Mac, in short, was commenting on for me. I say that prophets are criminals: even while they're alive as well as when they're dead, commentators take over their message. I bless my suffering. Hunger or thirst or the loss of the notion of time not withstanding, I am convinced that I have never left my African soil—or that I have already gone back there. I have seen nothing, learned nothing, and loved nothing.

If I am able to comprehend at all, beyond words, beyond forced ideas, beyond recollections of a previous existence, my broken bones, my macerated flesh and my soul barely born and still undefined, do exist—in a kind of immobility that is astonished, detached, and independent of space and time. Mac's voice (I suppose that it's his) recalls to me, less by what it says than in the way that it is said—a chopper mincing parsley on a cutting board—that a North African named Waldik had existed, had wanted to play Gandhi or Tarzan in Europe, and had ended up swallowing five grams of sleeping pills. He tells me his history with the clear, simple logic of a European, a man of letters, a political journalist who specializes in North African matters. Meanwhile as I listen to him, hear him, and comprehend without assimilating (abstractions do not touch me), the memory of another voice comes to mind, a voice that issued forth from a combination of duckcloth, calcified cap, and a pair of out-sized shoes. That voice had used the same words and the same ideas, but not with the same meaning.

When all is said and done, Mac O'Mac's face is like a mist. I look at him through it. I look at him with little shoeshine-boy eyes. A legion of flies blankets them, but I have not yet learned to consider them a sociological problem. And I see a European in his shirt sleeves who is perspiring, talking, gesticulating. I don't like those restless movements. I wonder just what it is about that Arabo named Waldik that affects him. He could push him out the door and wipe away his sweat. But later on I was to learn that his dignity as a specialist in the problems of North Africa would have suffered. And I still would not be able to comprehend, because it is my own story, and it does not touch me.

I remember now, but that is all that I can do. Like that European, I perspired, gesticulated, and hollered. I even wept. Other masks people and haunt my brain, but at present they are my own. Annihilating Mac O'Mac, I examined them. At best, I know that that was the state I was in. Much later on, at Tizi Ouzou in the market square, I see myself acting as a public storyteller. For the edification of soldiers in from the countryside, and donkeys, recounting my own story.

She had opened the door and stood there in the diffused light of morning. She shivered. Slender. I could have said: inoffensive.

"Beat it."

I got dressed, put on my shoes, and buttoned my old military jacket.

"Where can I go?"

She didn't blink an eye.

"Out . . . anywhere . . . but get out!"

Once a long time ago, hands together, I had held her face as once I held the hand of my mother, as one holds a cup that one has just created: that face will have no expiration, no idiom, fashioned in my faiths and baked in the oven of my hopes.

"I am leaving."

Suddenly it was a face I did not recognize. We had lived together for a long time, but black soap is a strong detergent.

I had gone down the steps. I had stopped at the bottom. "Can you lend me 200 francs?" My steps still resounded in the air, in the naked trees, in the morning light, in the nightgown that trembled against her legs (or was it her legs that were trembling?), and in my voice. They were like the tolling of an iron bell, soft, timid, and derisive. "I'll be glad to give you 200 francs, but get out of here!" The air was cold. There was hardly any wind. A bird—it was a blackbird—sounded two notes.

I reclimbed the stairs two hours later. I shoved the door open with my knee and stood on the threshhold.

She was standing up with a wet apron in her hand that was dripping drop by drop into the gray puddles on the floor.

"I came back . . ."

There was a strong odor of perfume in the air.

". . . to see you one last time."

She was wearing shorts. The look in her eyes was peculiar, a renouncement.

"I said to myself that perhaps you had not really thought about it, that you had just been very angry: I've swallowed my pride."

She did not move, did not blink an eye. Nothing is as dead as a being who has ceased loving.

I put the sleeping pills into my mouth one by one, like chick-peas. I was standing up, rigid, soulless, and began to chew them methodically. I was conscious of the fact that this act later on, in the opinion of a staid and stolid critic, would be the action of a paranoiac: lives must make an impression and cause comment to be taken seriously. Later on I would also have the occasion to read the novelized life of Joan of Arc and would understand then what one means by developing anxiety, all that remains of Christ except for the Cross. She dropped the apron and cried out that she didn't want any trouble. She'd had enough already, that she was just a poor soul that wanted nothing but a little peace. There were other parts of France or of Algeria to die in. I had to choose her house just to annoy her, to make a spectacle of myself even in dying. She had just phoned Mac O'Mac, and he was waiting for me. As for her, no thanks, she wanted nothing more to do with writers or with Arabs. Then she called for help.

Standing in my duckcloth trousers and my old military jacket, I watched her cry out, and kept on chewing, balancing myself on the balls of my feet. It was like chewing and swallowing every cry she made. Footsteps, and then a cloud of voices, drew nearer. Above my head, the sky was lowering and heavy, so heavy that I threw the empty vial toward it, and so low it must have struck it.

The air was more humid that cold. Somewhere in the gray sky, there was a gray spot that must have been the sun. Strong arms had taken hold of me and were pulling me backwards. I let myself be pulled. She was still standing on the steps, dressed in an old sweater that clung to her body as tight as skin, and a pair of shorts that left her almost naked. I looked at her soft, milky legs. My last effluvia were for them, into them. I had stroked them so often. They were my childhood dreams, my memories, the hair of my mother that I used to caress.

Suddenly right beside her stood Rauss. He smiled, panting, sweating like a greyhound standing there. She didn't even have the strength left to cry out or to close the door and get away. He stood there for a moment, not moving, with his lips drawn back, the greyhound, tossing her knife from one hand to the other. She opened her mouth, and he walked toward her.

I still don't know if I dreamed or just imagined it. The sleeping pills were already taking effect, so that I was not at all concerned. I know the extraordinary staying-power of my body that could fast indefinitely and digest a meal of vipers. Five grams of sleeping pills were like a bludgeon to it, but it needed them. I watched. That was all I was capable of doing.

It was like something happening years before, and that I was witnessing on a day I felt depressed. The arms had let go of me. They were gesticulating on the steps, thumping and confused in a formless swarm. A human cluster had formed around Rauss, but he stood there as solid as a rock. I could see his head, lined with shadows and jutting with angles, looking like something carved out of tin-plate. He was shouting verses of the Koran. I knew what that meant. Not that he was in danger, but because he was going to act. With one hand over the heads of his assailants, holding a knife in it that he was brandishing like a priest with a holy-water sprinkler. Without violence and methodically, he was twirling it in a series of quick thrusts, slashing at the verses with obscenities, his teeth yellow and sharp. For an instant, he seemed to weaken, but it was only a ruse. He pushed the human swarm away from the steps with a strong and sudden blow. He stood there alone with Simone, his hand still holding the belt of her shorts. He had stopped his litanies and was looking at her. But it was as if he were looking not at her but at me. As if he had wiped out, written off and printed, generations of repressions, of love, of enthusiasms, and of benedictions through this woman who despised him so. He has been frustrated so deeply for so long, before even birth, that even I could not fully grasp it. "In the name of God," he chanted. Then there were two knife strokes, two flashes, and the shorts fell to the ground, cut to ribbons.

But that's only the way it was. The only thing left of my drama was a pair of shoes. I looked at them. They were black, and they were laughing. Eight years in France, five of them in prison, three between two prison gates; a grandiose dream and death by gangrene. Imprisoned in a single woman, an Arabo's love. Things will always be that way. The cow and the lamb will be slaughtered and turned into meat to be sold and eaten, and their bones into glue or bleaching agents. The memory of the beast may be long since gone, but the leather will last. Nothing is lost for man.

I would never tell people who have stayed in Africa that the mirage of Europe eats like a tapeworm, to send their shoes instead of themselves. The only thing an Arabo can do in Europe is to walk—in search of happiness; nor would I tell them that a date-palm atrophies there and dies far less of the frost than of the restrictions: of air, of life, of space, of time, of sun, of love—as does a child of the soil made of flesh, bone, and instincts (and of nothing else); or, first of all, to bring their own air, their own space, their own sun . . .; none of the propaganda of book, of periodical, or of philosophy is worth any more than this: the affirmation that comes from doubting. No, I would not tell them any of that. They have different eyes from mine, different nerves, different good will. There might come a time of understanding and even of mercy.

I do not see myself as the representative of any person or thing whatsoever, except myself. Even those who love me—Rauss and the Butts—have always considered me a stranger, a case apart. But, good Lord, how I have learned to love what I was once.

This person who is talking and pacing and breathing in air like someone asphixiated is only, if I still know how to count on my fingers, shining my shoes. He is talking about forms of writing and novelistic techniques, cites a quotation from *The Holy Family,* his first novel, and the coercive, psychic, which means atmospheric, circumstances that made it a success. He hammers me with figures and facts about the insolence of editors, about library cards, and the French public. He says it is the strangest in the world, precisely because strictly speaking there is no public opinion. Whether leitmotif or steam-hammer, invariably he ends what he says with *The Holy Family,* and he starts with it too. Taking it all together, whatever I am now or have been, or have wanted to be or to communicate, the Butts and their misery, Africa and the rest of the world, other writers either dead or to come, God and paradise, the metempsychoses and the saints, even the concept of chance and the fifth dimension of Einstein, cornered, crushed, pulverized by these enormous bull-dozers of novels of Mac O'Mac, it all has the effect on me of the yawning of a toad. I lifted my head for the first time and looked at Mac O'Mac.

It was not that his face was soft or cowardly or hazy. It wasn't even that his skin was flabby covering flabby flesh and cartilage instead of bone, nor even that one could distinguish skin, flesh, bones, as might be expected in a human face—but because you might say that the whole head (hair and glasses included) looked like something that had been meticulously boiled.

At any rate, I got to my feet and stretched out my arm, clutched at the air, and turned toward the door. I remember that I was smoking a cigar; I don't know how or when I stuck it between my teeth. All I recall is that it gave off a bitter smell as though it were a piece of string I was smoking.

With a shove, he turned me toward him. He took my cigar and threw it on the floor, then mashed it with his heel. I saw his eyes.

"Do you have a passport?"

Behind his glasses, his eyes were singularly flat and lifeless, like two disks of plastic fitted into their orbits.

"Yes. Why do you ask?"

He turned around and called out:

"Minette! . . . Mi-nette!"

Then he explained to me over his shoulder: "Madeleine, my wife, old chap. Be courteous."

I picked up the cigar, rolled it back into shape, and lit it again.

"You have the passport with you?"

"Yes."

There appeared a stick-like figure surmounted by thirty-two teeth over which chastely and quickly had been thrown a calico dress, thin, flimsy, and with gestures like broken twigs. I could give her no weight, no age, not even presence or name. She held out the end of her fingers to me, five matchsticks, which I shook.

"Missioo," said Minette.

"Minette," said Mac, "this is Waldik, an Arab who wants to write books."

"Missioo," repeated Minette.

"I am a kind of missionary," Mac went on, "and pity is a consideration. Just like Christian charity." He cracked the joints of his fingers and added: "I am going to buy him a plane ticket and then I hope I hear nothing more about him."

"Missioo," concluded Minette.

Then disappeared.

From that moment on, I remember nothing at all. If my eyes saw and my ears heard, then I left one and the other at Mac's office. If it is a warehouse of furniture and pottery, or a household ready for moving that we passed through, one behind the other, shaking hands with the Arabs (who got to their feet cautiously and sat back down very quickly, with their Gestapo dossiers under their arms, their papers of expropriations and of infinite hope, sitting like a line of bowling pins on a set of benches that lined the walls of the vestibule) and whispered to them that they will be glad to wait for him or to come back later. I was clicking my heels together and staring at the bald rosy back of his head that looked like a monk's tonsure. I made no judgment.

When I arrived a while ago, I understood nothing and wanted to understand nothing. In short, those sons of Arab villages carrying oriental vases, Arab furniture, rugs or clusters of dates, who were shown in by a jovial secretary and whom Mac did not even look at, I took for real furniture movers. I could establish no relationship between their burdens and these patient soliciters, seated in the hallway. Mac O'Mac is the representative of these poor souls, and his name is known in the humblest shack in the remotest mountains of Algeria. They know, and I now know too, that one must never speak directly, that if some thirty million North Africans suffer and wait, it is not for them to express themselves, but for a Mac O'Mac to do it for them. Diet of dates or jug of wine in hand, the exploitation of suffering and of human hope, and, at the same time, the affirmation of the precious political and literary personality of Mac O'Mac, what is the worth of a moral principle? They have given their love of men at bay to him with complete impulsiveness, and he does not even recognize it. He's the one I feel sorry for.

As far as I'm concerned, fine! This self that is going to leave, that has nothing more to look forward to in France, I am going to provide him with something more that just a bunch of dates in exchange for the airplane ticket he is so ready to purchase for me. I'm ready to leave him my inheritance in France: even Simone and my son. And even the Butts! And my memories and my little moments of happiness. My experiences. A literary bastard! He could get a novel out of it, a mistress, a little shoeshine boy, whatever he wants—even if these notions continue to be like knots of suffering in my gullet. He has the style and the ease and the mixture of a businessman, completely patented and with official recognition of public services.

"God!" I said out loud, "deliver me from my past."

He was more smiling that snickering. The wind is playing in his cornsilk wisps of hair, in his clothes, in the threads of his yellowish and steely saliva, for his mouth was half open. As it blows the half-folded canvas of his Cadillac convertible parked in the lot at the airport, all style and ease.

I am on the other side of the barricade, but it is not Mac I am looking at. The plane revs its motors, a loudspeaker booms, the wind comes and goes like a caressing breeze. I know that this is the hour of my final choice, that all of my being, my *self,* is in the balance for the greatest freedom—but the little Berber boy I see upsets me deeply.

"Roasted peanuts . . . pistachios . . . peanuts . . ."

His voice is shrill, as shrill as his soul! He has put down the basket that earns his daily crumbs and looks at me, glued to the barricade as though he wished that that barricade were the tails of my army jacket! He has no need to say anything, nor do I. Two birds have touched feathers, one wounded and going back to the nest, the other barely an abortion, so very frightened in this strange land. Watch over and take care of your wings, save your wheat, and suffer in silence. Be humble, be full of love even toward those who belittle you and make fun of you. You will soar into the air, and you will know prison and hunger, you will know cold and misery in soul and body. Eaten by your wretchedness and cowering in it like a rat in its hole, even your compatriots will exploit you and degrade you. Unless you grow some pectorals, and evil bores into you, then you will be the one who will exploit others. But above all, do not lose your soul.

Oh, says the soul of the little Berber boy to me, my father, kiss my father's hand. You will find him sitting on a rock at the turn in the road. He has no land anymore, no arm anymore, no faith to keep him going. Tell him I sent him a money order yesterday for a thousand francs. Tell him I'm just fine and that France is the land of plenty . . . To my mother, don't say anything. Just kiss her feet for me three times.

I ran toward the plane so I wouldn't jump back over the barricade and strangle the child. An arm got me up the ramp, and the sound of the motors became a veritable cataract of noise and of tears, and the wind gusts and there was this child down there with his neck and his soul so thin and his basket at his feet and glued to the barricade frail before all of Europe—what an absolute this Europe is for all of us!

As I was being pushed toward the cockpit, I turned around and stiffened.

Above the head of Mac that was still snickering, toward that confident child who was already dead, I threw my shoes.

He would certainly have need of them!

PART TWO

IMPRIMATUR

1

The Algerian Airlines Comet came down quietly at Le Bourget. It glided along the runway without a sound and stopped in front of the airport, fresh and ready, without a single vibration or shortness of breath or fatigue. You would not have thought it had gone through space at 900 kilometers an hour. At the very second it landed, it seemed ready to take off again, an eagle in a torrent of metal.

One passenger stayed behind. He was dressed in a suit of light linen. Spare and thin, he was shivering in the brisk morning air, a pipe clutched in his teeth, hair blowing in the wind. His eyes had no life to them—and on his face, no sign of emotion. He does not feel the wind that bites him. Far off, very far away, almost a dream against the horizon stretching in front of him, the first signs of dawn begin to glitter. As if day had just been born or was having trouble in its birth, with the gleams that were its parturition pains.

He stands there on the pavement straining toward the horizon. He has no more hatred in him. He still feels a sudden tendency to bitterness, but nothing more. Life is before him, in him, in this pavement, in the wind that strikes him. His past is wiped away, dead, something that never existed, and he knows that on the horizon it is he who will finally be born.

Yalaan Waldik lights his pipe and walks toward the airport.

2

Sepia, bistre, and cinnabar.

The sun had come up, set, had illuminated nothing, warmed nothing, not so much as the skeleton of an Arabo, in a static and cold November sky, hardly more dead than an eye out of its socket, and as bloody.

Sepia, bistre, and cinnabar. The acuteness did not come from tactile or painful sensitivity. And not even fitting to objects. Nor were the tones intrinsic, existing in an absurd way, like pots of paint absurdly forgotten and then rediscovered there. It was simply that there at the open door, they had struck his eyes like a fist blow. He stood there for a moment, framed in the doorway—and he said to himself that he was surely wrong, that he had awaited this moment like a deliverance, and that, after all, it was just a question of an exasperated sensitivity. So intensely that absurd colors had been created *behind* his retina.

He seemed dehumanized speaking in third person, with such lucidity that he wondered if that dehumanization were not more of a splitting of personality that had taken place several weeks earlier, that early morning, for example, when Simone had driven him out of that room on whose threshhold he was now standing. Where he could even see himself at that very moment, sitting at the table smoking, excitedly talking like cast-off clothes that had been forgotten and then found again, and that he was going to put back on with emotion.

But it was much further back in time, and much more vivid and absurd. Those several boards planed down, nailed together and painted, had constituted the first door open to him in France. He would always remember it. He had opened it with a total absense of doubt.

Forty-eight pairs of Arab eyes stung him like as many swords' points. They stripped him down, picked him apart, and assessed him in a fraction of a second that was longer than eternity—forty-eight pairs of eyes just as quickly extinguished and lowered, dejected. He went in because an octopus-like arm grabbed hold of the epaulette of his jacket and his shoulder, his past and his future earnings, his tares and his avatars, all sorts of obligations and possibilities—a tatooed Arab hand weighted down with rings. Quietly he loosened the grip, a finger at a time, then looked first at the hand and then at the man who was smiling at him with all his thirty-two gold teeth.

"Call me 'boss.' How much you got on you?"

He clicked his jaws one against the other, like the clank of the guillotine.

"How much money?" he repeated.

"Very little," said Waldik.

"Boss!"

"Very little, boss."

"Hand it over."

He gave it to him. He still had no doubts. He was eighteen years old, and only his glands were pubescent. All around him he heard mocking laughter, sounds of salivation and of sniffling. His throat began to choke from the oder of humid dirty underwear.

He handed him the handkerchief that his mother had embroidered for him, pressing it flat with her fingertips and perfuming it with jasmin. He had knotted it around several silver coins and two or three banknotes: the amount his father got from selling his last goat.

"You're right," said the man. "It's not very much. Follow me."

He gave back the handkerchief. Then with an index finger as sharp as a bayonet in his back, shoved him from behind down a corridor that was lit by a cellar window and smelled of saltpeter. Another hand grabbed Waldik by the shoulder and led him into a room that was similar to the first one, furnished with a bench and a chair. A prodigious number of Arabs, seated on the bench, looked at him and then lowered their heads as had the first group. Still others were squatting about or stretched out on the floor on newspapers. They looked at him too and did not take their eyes off him. The one who held him by the shoulder had jumped up from his chair like a triggered coilspring.

"Call me 'foreman.' "

"Fine, foreman. I gave everything I had to the boss."

The foreman let go of him, then emptied the newcomer's pockets, and took his tie. He put everything he found in a kind of pouch that hung over his stomach. Then he jammed his thumb into his back and directed him down another corridor.

Waldik went down it as he had the first one. The second one smelled of sulphur. Then he recalled that the room he had just left smelled of pruritus. He had no puberty left, not even sexual.

When, much later, he ended up before the triple chin of a European, he had nothing left but his shirt, his pants, and his shoes. Even his shoelaces had been plundered: a tip, they had told him. That's the way it is here. Move! Quick!

He stood for a while in front of the triple chin and the white wood table piled high with papers. Now and then he would glance down at the copper tag that he had been given. "Be sure not to lose it," the sub-sub-foreman had warned. "If you do, you'll have to go back to Africa for more tips." He looked at it. 302, the square tag said. It was smaller and dirtier than the shoeshine tag he had had at home in Tizi-Ouzou. He looked at it with a mixture of fear and stupor. "Did I come all the way across the sea to take up shoeshining again?" he wondered.

Then the European raised his eyes and looked at the tag.

"What number?"

"302, Monsieur Commissioner," said Waldik.

"Tomorrow," said the man, who opened a drawer, took out a bottle of beer, uncapped it, and drank it down, all of it, it seemed to Waldik, in one single gulp, the way you take a shot at an outlaw just by pressing on a trigger.

"Monsieur Commissioner . . ."

The man threw the empty bottle down behind him.

"Tomorrow, I said. Now, move on."

The next morning Waldik was there. At dawn. The processing

center was closed. As if misery existed only during office hours. He who sleeps, eats, says the proverb, "and he who dies during the night is still dear to me," added Waldik aloud. Consequently he took off his shoes and pounded on the door. He hammered it methodically, first with the heel and then with the toe, then his hands, his fists, his back, as though he were already pounding against his future dog's life. He wasn't thinking of anything. He wasn't feeling anything. Tomorrow, the Christian had told him. Very well! It was tomorrow already, but which tomorrow? And how to find out? There was no landmark either in time or in space, in neither sky nor sun. The twilight of the previous evening looked exactly like this dawn, both of them gray, cold, and dismal. The only touchstone was the door that the "boss" had slammed behind him the night before. Since then, his eyes had not left it for a moment. He had backed away from it until his back struck a tree trunk and was welded to it. Not moving a finger, not even shivering, throughout the night in the light of a streetlamp, he stood watching the door.

It finally opened, and he dropped his shoes to the ground and stuck his feet into them. It opened with a torrent of curses, and revealed a swollen head and the blade of a kitchen knife. Waldik bent down and rammed his head into something soft. Then he straightened up, grabbed the knife, and closed the door.

"Good morning, boss," he said. "302. Number 302."

He wasn't angry yet. He said to himself that when the day of the reign of anger came, then he would know what despair was. No. He wasn't cold or hungry or thirsty. A meager misunderstanding, that's all. As thin and pugnacious as a dervish. He stood up completely and broke the blade of the knife with a quick twist of the wrist.

"302, boss," he said. "Where is the commissioner? Do you think a man from Tizi-Ouzou is nothing more than a number?"

On that swollen head, the eyebrows and the hair of the beard had stiffened. There weren't any eyelashes at all, just two sort of buttonholes of yellowish flesh over two black buttons, oval and shining, that were his eyes.

"Nine o'clock," said the boss without opening his mouth.

He raised and lowered his head like a truncheon. The gold and jewels of his rings sparkled.

"Offices don't open until nine o'clock, Arabo," he yelled bitterly.

"All right, Arabo," said Waldik.

He shoved him aside as you'd shove a beggar on the arms and shins. He dashed into the corridor, pursued by a chorus of insults. By the time he got out of the "commissioner's" office, the "boss" was already there, armed with a flat-iron.

"Nine o'clock, Arabo," he whispered in a soft voice.

Waldik looked at him for a moment. It seemed he was opening his eyes for the first time since he had arrived in France. He contemplated him with care, like a bull he'd been told to slaughter: hybrid nose and moustache, the skin the color of ashes and saffron, the glottis of a bird, the hollow torso, the twig-like legs and arms . . . and the look of distress, incommensurate and unhealthy, that he had never even seen in a reptile. Maybe he's a Pole, he thought, maybe a serf from the Middle Ages or a toad standing there with a human face. He surely was not an Arab from our part of the world. Then he closed his fist and sniffled—and there was a short fight.

Lying on the floor with the flat-iron for a pillow, Waldik had his eyes wide open. The smells of sulphur and of saltpeter had no doubt evaporated with the night, and an odor of ancient human flesh, of worm-eaten ruins and of stagnant water moved across the ground, like a draught of air. My future odor, he said to himself, but in how many years? How many years of distress will I have to live to be promoted to "boss"?

The "commissioner" stepped over him at noon, sweeping him with his feet as though they were a pair of brooms, but before he could get his door shut, Waldik was there standing in front of him, with his copper tag held out at arm's length. The man looked at him without anger or pity. The "commissioner" had long been nothing more than a mass-man. He had no faith except in Law and no opinions except for Regulations. He wasn't a bad man or even a particularly dumb man. He was a man of some fifty years, well-fed on cabbage and beer, and who had been stuck in the administration the way you stick away a file of papers. He hardly ever brought up the matter any more of the only and very aged lion he had once shot in his adventurous youth (because even he had been young once and had spent some time in the "bush") and he lived for nothing but his projection into the future: his retirement, and the little home with a red tile roof and a sunny garden plot that he had seen and made a payment on in the suburbs, and where he would finally be able to live quietly with his memories of the old lion.

He looked at Waldik. With his face of a savage and his arm held out and his copper tag, he was framed by the doorway like a standing portrait—one that could be cut out with a knife and hung up on the gates of the Ministry of French Overseas Affairs.

"Come on in and close the door. Give me your tag and sit down," he said.

Yes: those people still have faith. They don't know what convention is, and for them even a serial number is a feeling.

"Name? Given names?"

"Waldik, Yalaan."

"Born presumably in?"

"I don't know," said Waldik. "Am I a function of time? Here I haven't been born yet."

"No comments. You don't know how old you are?"

"No, but if it's to get a job, you can say I'm forty. The flesh is there, and it's solid." (Waldik flexed his biceps.)

"All right," said the other. "Born where?"

"Tizi-Ouzou, Algeria."

"How d'you write that?"

"Tizi-Ouzou. Where I live you don't write it. You just say it."

"No comment," yelled the 'commissioner'.

He filled out three forms in triplicate, posted the numbers of the writs in a ledger, scribbled on a piece of blue cardboard, and held it out to Waldik.

"Here's your unemployment card," he said to him noncommitally.

"Unemployment?" whispered Waldik. "Unemployment card? Tell me, Monsieur Commissioner, what am I supposed to do with it?"

"Have it punched every week. That's obligatory. Nothing else. Off now! Quick! Out with you! Next one!"

No doubt some time had passed since Waldik had gotten up and quietly put his chair in place. Other Arabs had come in and gone out, thin and emaciated, so much alike that they all put on the same drab, faded mask, with one more punch in their unemployment card that they carefully put away in their wallet, folded over and tied shut, before they went out. Once through the door, it seemed he could almost hear them live: all their surliness, all the negation of their life bursting forth in a veritable rosary of insults. He stood there for quite a while, holding his rectangle of blue cardboard, changing it from one hand to the other, turning it over and upside down, weighing it and sniffing at it until finally he understood. Then he went up to the man.

"Monsieur Commissioner . . ."

"What? M'name's Dupont. You still here? Get out!"

"Monsieur Commissioner Dupont, are you making fun of me?"

Dupont stood up. He went around his desk and put his arm around Waldik's shoulder, steering him gently toward the door.

"Listen to me, young man. Don't be a troublemaker. I can assure you that . . ."

Then he saw Waldik's eyes. They had suddenly gone dead, like someone anesthetized. Dupont had hardly taken his arm from his shoulder when Waldik jumped into the air and landed on the balls of his feet, crouching, a trapped animal, cornered and bruised, it seemed to him, but still with a little spark of life, the only thing he could defend and savagely hold on to, and worth a strength capable of cutting four men with four rifles into pieces—haggard, panting for breath, his muscles twitching and his teeth grinding together, he was shaking with rage at this mockery devised by a man placed (for he could not be a part of his activities) on the edges of society like a kind of residue: the mockery of the rectangle of cardboard that you had to have to be in proper standing in a society that rejected you and that you could just as well frame on the wall like the image of a saint.

"I ate it," said Waldik, syllable by syllable. "I ate my unemployment card. But it didn't give me any nourishment. I need a kilo of them a day, and I'll be here every God-created day to demand a kilo of unemployment cards. That's how many I'll need."

"Yes," thought Dupont, who had gone back to his seat and was pressing his hips tightly against the chair arms as though he thought the whole thing would turn into a blanket with which to cover himself up to the eyeballs. "They're all the same. Statistically nothing I can do. All I want is my retirement annuity."

"Yes," said Waldik, "there are even posters." He was still crouching on the floor and was talking very softly, almost to himself, as though he were trying to put himself to sleep. "Billboards with posters in our good old city of Algiers for the benefit of those poor dumb Arabs that announce in big red letters that workers are needed in France, that democracy abounds in France, that all you have to do is go down to such-and-such an agency and they'll even pay your trip . . . When I went to the agency, they wanted some money down, so I got across the sea in my own way: in a tar-barrel. The result was the same. Your boss and your colleagues all got their money down. The only difference was that they took everything except the last clothes on my back."

"Who? What? How can I know such things? Eh? Listen: do you want me to make a complaint?"

"Does a complaint here go the same route a request for work does?" continued Waldik. "Listen, why don't you just say right out that there are 10,000 Arabs walking around with unemployment cards and that I'm the last in line?"

"100,000." said Dupont sharply. "And they keep on coming by the bundle, and I'm sick and tired of it."

He uncapped a bottle of beer, drank it down, and tossed it behind him.

"Listen," he said vehemently, "You were in Algeria just a short while ago. Do you think they're all going to come here to France? At any rate, they're capable of moving up my age for retirement."

"Yes, all of them," said Waldik.

He got up off the floor and went over to sit on one side of the desk.

"Every young man with a pair of arms, guts and life that wants to find work and is fed up with misery and has grown up with faith in France and doesn't want to lose all hope and doesn't want to die. What age limit are you talking about?"

"Oh, nothing," said the 'commissioner' with a sigh, "the story of a lion."

He locked his beer drawer with a key and got to his feet. He was tottering.

"Listen, young man, don't come back tomorrow."

He pushed him ahead, straight out to the sidewalk, where they found themselves in the gray of twilight or of dawn.

"Don't ever come back," he yelled. "There is no work. No lodging. No help. No fraternity. There are only copper tags and forms to fill out and unemployment cards and promises. Nothing else. And me, I'm just an old goatskin full of fat and beer stuck to the flank of the bureaucracy."

Night had fallen some time before. It was raining a kind of wet, energyless, odorless and colorless depression, the drizzle of winter's night. When it finally stopped, Waldik lifted his head and felt something in the palm of his hand. He opened it and remembered. He had not even been angry. He now knew everything that he could expect from this life: a few crumbs. He tore up the money that Dupont had put in his hand when he left. He tore it up piece by piece, without shame but fully cognizant of the biting shame that that fat man must feel and take on himself, that man looking back on the full and intense life he had once been capable of, and toward which he had started out, the shame of doing nothing himself for years now. He tore the money in two, four, in eight, in sixteen, in thirty-two pieces. Then he strewed the bits into the stream of rainwater running down the gutter.

He knew that his future life would be like that too, leftovers, drifting. Time would take it upon itself to compromise his principles, and his faith would disappear. One day he would no longer be able to go back home at all, so empty of all substance and belief in the face of those Arabs who still held to their beliefs—but he did not have their faith.

Later on he would remember that first door that he had opened with such hope, like all the others that he would open . . . The leftover scraps of his life drifting in time like the distant scraps of money that had floated rudderless down the gutter.

He carefully closed the door. He knew that his smile had dissolved, and his good will had died.

"Good evening," he said.

3

She was alone. Seated on the bed, she was not startled or even surprised. She smiled and went on polishing her fingernails with a chamois skin.

"Good evening," she said.

The smile was too perfect, born too inopportunely in eyes and on lips that had no damn need for it. A clown's smile, and the back and forth of the chamois became more intense as though the nails she was polishing—and the palm, the wrist, the arm, the shoulder—were suddenly and simultaneously seized with the convulsive movement of a connecting rod.

She got up, took his valise from him, grasped him by the hand, and had him sit down beside her, carried away by her own little game and gratuity. Then she smoothed his hair with her painted and still spasmodic nails. She continued to believe that one person could bring about another's redemption.

"I came on board a Comet. Fantastic! Hardly more than an hour and a half ago."

You should have sent me a telegram," she complained gently. "Did you have any dinner?"

"Yes, of course."

Her eyelids rigid, set in cement, aimed her sight in a certain direction immutably fixed. All emotion, humility or pardon, that he longed for with the sharpness of a blow, was beyond him.

"I won't stay long," he said. He heard her voice, biting.

"Why?" said Simone.

She had let go of his hand. Her fingers apart, her palms against her temples, she looked at him, with a trembling smile on her lips: people who do not comprehend, smile.

"Why? You're in a hurry, are you?"

He rejected that also, that note of weakness that could have been a springboard toward a new departure. The sun had come up and set again. Several times. During two months. Everything had been decisive and in vain since that morning in September. He had seen nothing rise or set, as though time, the order of the world and human evolution had marched on without him. *First of all,* his predicament. During these last two months, he had ground it to pieces, like a hunk of mutton in other times, not even ground it up, but like something viscous from the beginning, a grinding that neither prolonged nor short could render sticky. He had caressed it like a dead bird, knowing full well that it was neither bird nor death—stubborn in the fixation of the moment and the rejection of all the vast rest that he called tears or earthquake, his pride came through it all cured, only his pride that had neither accepted nor comprehended, a quivering pride that had finally boarded a Comet to take things up where he had left them—and if there were accounts to settle, he would settle them in relation to pride, that tremulous wound, and the wound and the pride were precisely those two lost months.

"Shall I make some coffee for you?"

The palliative would have been something new for him. Strong and beautiful. Instead of that, he had seen his father, the beggar on the road. His father's face. Which he always knew was wrinkled. But not quite to such a degree. There are wrinkles which are a kind of penalty. Others which explain nothing at all, simply wrinkles and nothing more. His father's were from smallpox. Thin deep lines that cut into the face with such cruelty that he wondered when he had had smallpox. And what terrible kind of smallpox.

"I'd like a cup of coffee."

He had carefully counted the wrinkles of that face as you might a fig onto a string of figs or one empty day onto another, and he had added them to his thousand ancient little miseries.

"Very strong," he said. "Very strong coffee."

She got up and moved out of his sight into another room, and then came back. The dull sound of her bare feet on the cement floor announced her presense. He wished he were dead, embarrassed by his own existence, by the duty to reproduce himself. The sound recalled the two mosquitos killed between two hands. He smelled an odor of coffee, *an authentic odor of dead mosquitos,* thought Waldik. A presence and an odor of weak flesh, gratifying and always to gratify, an ordinary woman among millions of ordinary women who asked for nothing more than an ordinary life.

"I didn't sugar it," she began.

He put down the cup, grabbed her wrists, and held them in his hand. He got to his feet and looked at her. Everything inside his head was cement (he carressed her with his other hand: of cement!), even his eyes, except for a tiny pinpoint of a hole that was the pupil. She repeated: sugar . . . no sugar . . . sugar . . . As though from repetition, from the simple fact of repeating syllables, something would be born, a word or a sudden lethargy: not that she was afraid of being afraid; she loved fear as she loved her weakness, but there was a tragic hardness in this bone structure that he held by the wrists, a hardness that went beyond her, that was incomprehensible and hateful to him, for nothing was more detestable to him than apprehension and potential. She was satisfied to repeat syllables, not even euphonic ones, conscious of a kind of trinity that was one and divided at the same time: Waldik's eyes, hard and cold, his hand that was bruising her wrists and was even harder than eyes—there was in her, possibly, no coldness, but this hardness made her feel that she had to be cold, colder than the coldness of those eyes of his—and her own voice that was like a record stuck in one spot and saying over and over, sugar . . . no sugar . . . sugar . . . just syllables, but ones that had become symbolic.

"WHY?"

And she never knew when or where or why this cry came out, or even who had screamed it. If indeed it had been Waldik who was now astraddle her stomach like a bird of prey with its wings spread out, lying on the bed demolished by this massive blow of a cry, hardly blinking, hardly frightened—if indeed it had not been something stored up inside this Arab kneeling on her stomach, a whole series of humiliations and capitulations vis-á-vis his conscience, if he had a conscience, and in any case, vis-á-vis his glands and cells, be they those of a monkey, would in neither case permit capitulation; if indeed, to be more exact, summarized in the form of an interrogation and in good French, it was not a question of a whole agglomeration of atrophies called Arabos, those from France and from Navarre, from Africa and from Asia, the dead ones and the ones still to come, those that no longer have a name, dropped into space and into time, the waste products of civilization on the march, unassimilated and therefore residual, ever since the eighth-century defeat of the Arab armies at Poitiers, dropped and prejudged, without hope of redemption, or even in plain language, or a cry of revolt.

"He grilled a steak for me," she said. "He offered me liqueurs and American cigarettes. (Without being aware of it, she had suddenly begun to talk in a loud voice, but in her mouth there was not so much as a bubble of saliva.) It was in a spacious villa he had just bought the day before. He walked from one room to another, picked up a casserole, a painting, rubbed his hands, closed a drawer, told me that 'Minette' had stayed at the stadium where she was working on some dresses and where he normally wrote pretty little novels for a paperback publisher, and sold junk. With a kind of opium denser and more heady than the music, I was overwhelmed with misery, with children's meningitis, with solitude, above all with solitude. Later on, my darling, later on . . ."

"Yes," said Waldik tenderly.

She pushed him away, using hands and feet, writhing on the bed with hiccups wet with tears, or near-tears or the desire for tears that would not come to her eyes. Above her head there was a lightbulb under a lampshade, a raw light that was almost physical.

"Yes," Waldik repeated.

There was a tenderness in his voice, in his eyes that now were wet and a little red, but that were also withdrawn like those of a man who had long since forgotten how to sleep. In his slow and calm gestures, above all, as though his nerves had been emptied of all influx, he had taken up a chair and sat down next to the bed. He looked like a growth on the side of it.

A mosquito had settled on his neck and was screeching like a rusty crane.

"I followed him into the bedroom. He was smoking a long thin cigar of a kind I had never seen before. He fluffed up some cushions and caressed some strange-looking vases—he said they were Etruscan, Byzantine, and Greco-Roman—then pushed some light switches. A wood fire crackled in the corner fireplace of mauve brick. He pressed his fingers into the seat where I was going to sit as though he were giving it a kiss, and, close to my eyes and my lips (he smelled of cigar, of cologne and of flesh), he recited the whole of an epic. I could see myself again as a child, feet cold and trembling with fear, in a nightshirt that swept along the floor of the long corridor, somber and cold. I was scratching at the door of my grandmother's house. I have never spoken to you of her, or of my childhood, or of my joys, as those things don't interest you, and I climbed up on her bed where she would tell me long tales about fairies, knights-errant, and vast spaces . . ."

"Yes," said Waldik bitterly.

He had neither brushed the mosquito away nor swatted it. He had simply moved it slightly, with a delicate and steady finger, to bite anew in another spot on his neck.

Neither the facts nor the manner of telling mattered to him. Neither sincerity nor repentance. He said to himself: "How could I have hated or even loved this woman who once was that child?"

"A whole modern epic," Simone went on. "He had seated me on his knees, but I was barely aware of it. It was only later that I became conscious of it. By then it was too late. It was an epic about writers and critics and editors, and how a whole literary technique had been substituted for Durandel's sword of earlier times, a new concept of honor for the old-fashioned one, a new tiltyard where traitors in the contemporary literary world, knights of the novel and all the rest that were their rascally counterparts jousted and fought; about awakenings, about taking a stand, about gall, and about colossal battles of polemics and of sanctions in the form of literary prizes. By the time I realized I was sitting on his lap, I also saw that he had turned out almost all of the lights. The room was all in half-tones, half-sighs, like my flesh and my heart. For an instant the reality but not the charm of it all, was almost destroyed when he told me that the next morning he would begin divorce proceedings. But he extinguished all compromise with his lips . . . oh, my darling, forgive me . . . I didn't know what I was doing . . ."

"Yes," said Waldik.

He was all cement again. *Yes: not even a man. Not even with his man's limbs and his man's glands.* He brushed away the mosquito. Then, as he thought of it, he got up, caught it, killed it, put the dead insect on the palm of his hand, sat down and then crushed it until there was nothing more than a brown spot on his hand. *Oh no, not even a man. Not even an old man who could try his old man's luck. But no! Literature had been sufficient.*

"Yes," he said in a hoarse voice, "yes . . . yes . . ."

Someone knocked at the door and opened it.

"Do you need anything, child?"

It was old Josepha, the neighbor, or simply her voice, her shadow as soon as she caught sight of Waldik. He got up and accompanied her back to her shanty, strolling along. He put her to bed and tucked her in, "No, the child has no need of anything." Then he went back to his seat beside the bed, and repeated:

"Yes . . . yes . . ."

One might have said that Simone, emaciated, cavernous, empty of all perception, had not even noticed, lying across the bed like an insect, with the submission and breathing of an insect. There were various objects in the room, a stool, a chair, a hearth-rug, engravings on the wall. A chest for firewood piled full. A ball of yarn with several rows of stitching and needles in it next to it. The debris of wealth and of joys, but therein was the symbol of his resurrection, of two months of new life: day after day, hope woven to hope, the nightmare had become hardly anything more than a name.

He was thinking: *almost well, My son was almost well.* He was thinking, not with his faculty for thought, but with his flesh, his wish for tears, his hands. He was thinking that there must have been underneath this bed where she was not even an insect: a diagram, an insect's role, underneath this floor where draughts of cold air blew as weak as a rat, good earth for hoeing and ready for the shovel of anyone who, like that earth, had remained a spark, a single hope, and who had believed and still believed, using that abstraction as starting point to live again, to reject and to play destiny, all apprehension of destiny, the very word itself. And then one evening that earth unexpectedly reappears in the human shape of an Arab. The world was as incomprehensible, as unpredictable, and as cloying as a fly on raw meat. He was thinking: *now he is going to die. I know that my son is going to die.*

She said:

"The room gave off tawny colors, whispered secrets. Mac had taken my hand and was caressing it. I looked into his eyes, almost drowning in them. Even now I couldn't tell you if they were blue or black. They were like a mirror . . ."

"Yes," said Waldik. "Yes. Yes. Yes."

His hands were resting against Simone's breast, but she did not feel them, hands rigid and heavy. The voice of the wind called down into the fireplace, a voice wounded and full of fear.

"Like a mirror," Simone went on, "a mirror in which I could see myself. Except that it was not my real image. In it I saw that Simone who still a little girl, partial to fairy tales and to epics. Life had not touched her with a single ugly moment. I could somehow feel a hand that was taking off my clothes and a warm mouth whispering in my ear. I had lost all sense of reality or time. As if a minute had not gone by since those evenings of my childhood. I had not had a child. I had never met an Arab. I had never gone hungry or been cold or felt misery in my soul. I had never been belittled. I had never gone outside of my little circle. I was that little ten-year-old."

She paused, seemed to be dreaming. Even her voice had taken on the frail sure intonation of little girls. Her breasts seemed flatter and her shoulders shrunken. Her neck had become slender and delicate. Waldik could feel it very well. One of his hands had run up the breast to the throat, but it had the bad temper, rigidity and the energy of a murderer's hand.

Simone vaguely felt a pressure and she looked at him. She

thought she was seeing a mask of wax hanging above her with two black, set, shining holes in it. Above the mask was an electric light. It was as though it had no existence. Cold, clean, incisive, of no help, without pity, or any soul. For a fraction of a second she thought she was going to burst into laughter at the idea of the term *reflexes.* It was as though she were already destined for oblivion.

"Yes," said Waldik.

As if she herself, for her own oblivion, had just woven a whole packet of cords. A Polack would have understood that those cords were knotted with suffering, but not an Arabo, not a Waldik.

She burst out laughing and it was a hooting laughter, bitter and very brief. It was more of a rattling in the throat than a laugh.

"Yes," cried Waldik.

She had been wrong. Inside of her, in the depths of her past, there was the face of a tense and very pale little girl. Now she could feel the hand on her throat, joint by joint and notch by notch, the five fingers of the Arabo who had been cuckolded. She had made a serious mistake, and the little girl seemed to be formulating a simple reproach: why had she ever had confidence in an Arabo?

"He undressed me and carried me over to the bed. Then he caressed me and kissed me. I gave myself to him . . ."

She had another burst of laughter, but it was one of defiance, of derision. You might as well say that everything, even the dream, was absurd.

"He's no good in bed," she said . . .

And she said nothing more. In the space of a thought, she saw, lying on a hospital bed, a child with flabby skin and a swollen stomach with a needle of a syringe stuck in his buttock and attached to a vial of physiological serum. The child gave a start and called out "Mother" two times. She knew that she was sobbing breathlessly and struggling violently against a burning mouth. And it was in a liquid fever that Waldik, with deep, implacable, metallic laughter, tore off her clothes and cried out, still laughing: ". . . what you are . . . I am going to take you for what you are . . ."

The wind still called out in the chimney, whispering restlessly, slightly shyly, as though surprised by the burst of sobs, laughter and voice. He cried out:

". . . I take you for what you are . . . and nothing else . . ."

The wind, later on, whispered alone.

4

But the sound of thumbnail hitting against tooth, nothing was either finished or defined—and those who think, philosophize and write, propose elements, solutions and systems, and examinations, of conscience and of Christianizations, those people have no doubt never seen Arabs and know nothing of their existence or of their soul. They have flown over them as one flies over a city, high above, comfortably fastened into a seat, their stomach full and their brain dulled with—in back of them, in front of them, inside of them—the mathematical postulate that they alone are the beginning and the end, the word and the approbation, that they alone know and live and will survive, that they alone possess truth and beauty, and that even the economy must be fashioned in their image. A single glance from a carpet vendor amazes them and, if they should reflect on it, it would kill in them all hope of satisfaction, all attempt at creating in the reality of fertilizers and of orgasms their reality of words and ideas. Life has no need of history and history has no need of books (instead, civilizations and centuries can be judged by their coinage). They would write of capitulations, of widowhood, of insolvency: and if there is a single one of them who dares to grumble, be it in the depths of an indulgence or even with a hint of indulgence, that person can expect my fist in his mouth. It may be that there are none among them, however, who still have all their teeth; a redemption, whether it is carnal, or Christian, cures nothing, redeems nothing, not even in the flesh. Even the term 'redemption' is an abomination. It belongs with the terminology of merchants and haggling. In the language of life, that *thing* has no name, does not really exist.

Rauss understood very well when he saw Yalaan come out shaking his fists, his feet, his head, his body, his teeth.

All that could be done was to start the car, to shift the gears and speed up, two gestures and two sounds of metal, as Waldik jumped onto the seat beside him, almost onto his lap. No one had shut the gate. There was none to shut.

What difference could it make and to whom, and to what, if the night was dark? Here and there like moist spots several haloes shone, but they were too dim to be more than obscure reflections changing in the misty air. Rauss and Waldik were not aware of mist or reflections or night. They drove along in their jalopy, a huge fresco born of another continent. With every turn of the wheel, they lost something of their bitterness and their edge; but the people who saw them pass by, an insensitive and soulless mass, would say they had noticed nothing at all, because to do otherwise would have meant facing their own bankruptcy.

The motor coughed and sputtered. Rauss was whistling an old tune, and they glided along the road with its cold wisps of fog that did not turn to water.

Half reclined in the seat, and wrapped in what had been a rug, light and threadbare in some places and stiff and heavy in others, Waldik felt the mute and ancient anger of the Arabs rising in his soul. It was still far off, like the crest of a distant wave, but he already felt its violence.

He felt that for years now he had been walking on his head instead of his feet, and that what he had used for footwear were studded soles that hurt badly. Or to be more exact, it was shoes that had walked on his head, had pressed, sounded, shaken and brushed away their dust. He also had a feeling, both vague and powerful, as a sensation, that out of the chain of his sufferings, if he ever stood on his two feet like everyone else, and on the heads of others like everyone else, all that would arise would be more suffering.

And he could not help but be moved, even though he understood that such feelings should be considered with reservation. Even though he had been told ten, twenty, a hundred times, that there were two kinds of feelings, those that were *civilized,* cultivated like a suburban householder's lawn and that could *create,* and those that were like his, chronic sentimentalities rooted in neurosis and usually treated in an asylum.

The radio! That was all he wanted. He had opened and closed a lot of doors—one belonged to a rug merchant who gave him carpets to sell. He did sell one: one winter's night he went into a café, threw down the rugs on the billiard table, and flopped down himself, so worn out that the woman who ran the place remembered that, even to a rug salesman, Christian charity could be shown. So she bought one from him, but before she did, she asked him for his papers, pointed out to him that he had no license to go around selling rugs, haggled more tenaciously than an Arab (she had gone on a ten-day tour to Corsica), and, with an air of quiet disinterest, told him that those rugs were ones that had been confiscated in customs and that he, Waldik, had stolen them from the customs officers. She pulled out the biggest and thickest rug of them all and into his pocket stuffed a francnote that was almost enough to pay for a sack of potatoes, gave him a glass of wine at the bar and said, here, drink this Ahmed. It'll put some life in you. He got up and drank it, but when he turned around to pick up his rugs, he saw the yellow teeth of a customer sitting at a table. Those teeth were full of scorn and mockery. Waldik picked up a wine bottle and knocked them in. That's when, for the first time, prison gates closed behind him—the gates of that prison he did not want to leave. He had done his time, but he was terror-stricken by the street and its noises and by all the problems he would have to solve again: food and drink and a roof over his head. He went back and begged the jailer to keep him there. He said that he had killed and stolen and raped, but the guard grabbed him by the shoulders and shoved him into the street. The next door he went through was a priest's, at midnight, without knocking. To the priest he exemplified Islam's hypocracy, but the Arab told him about his anxieties, which were sufficient to identify him with the anxieties of Christianity. He got a bowl of soup and a subway ticket. The next door was at the Algerian employment office. He went in with "Eureka" on his lips. "You're not disabled because of your job?" asked an Arab. "You don't have an incurable illness? You're not officially deported? Then we can't repatriate you. Out with you! Get out!"

A radio! Some days were vaster than the sea. Others were stillborn. He ate what he could find, slept where he could, sometimes found some work just by accident, gardener, hawker of porno photos, stevedore . . . He worked with an energy born of rage, as though for him, the work were not to fill his belly, nor to give him a momentary stability or even joy—but he always felt that it was a kind of trial run, like a bronze or a piece of granite out of which he was supposed to create a work of art, not even breathing, determined to show the persons who had hired him that they had been right to do so, to prove to them that if they wanted standard results, he would give them ten times that and that nothing, not even charity, could kill the man that was in him. One day the supervisor in a coal yard jostled him and took away his shovel. "You're going to break it," he cried. "Just what is this savage here?" And that's the way it was again and again. He could still remember the teachings of that Catholic from Bône: *God provides the food for the crows,* he had said. Yes, but Waldik was far from being a crow.

He thought he had found his salvation when he went down into the mines. What a good old mother the Earth was. Down in her innards, he buried himself with such peace! That same day, they found out that he didn't belong to a union and they sent him down to the very deepest parts, but he still thought he had been saved. He learned to handle a pick and the wagon, and to move around in a space the size of a rathole, to breathe a mixture of humidity, heavy gas and coal dust, but it was so peaceful! That hole was exactly what he needed and what he was breathing was just right for his lungs. A hopper took him back up. He rolled a cigarette and smoked it down to the tip. It wasn't that he was short of tobacco, but because it was the farewell cigarette that all the miners smoked: he kept it going, chatting with them, telling them about himself and Algeria, a beggar asking for human fellowship. They shook his hand without looking at him, convinced that he was a dog that worked with them in the mine, and off they went to their wives: modern warriors off for modern relaxation. There were a half-dozen Arabs with Waldik. They had no wives or any ties to the area: nothing more than a shack made of flimsy black boards and a stove they didn't know how to light, and cots that they avoided like the plague. They knew very well that sooner or later every night society forced them back among Arabs, stripped bare in front of one another like a group of castaways on a raft, with their terrible hunger for life—and that nostalgia for the soil of Africa that they did not talk about but which excited them all: black earth that broke into foam like a rising tide.

They went back to their shack as late as they could: waiting outside in the nordic mists, shivering, coughing, spitting, their teeth chattering, and smoking one cigarette after another. They were proud of the day's work each had done and of the tons of coal they had dug out of the earth . . . a kind of epileptic laughter, it seemed to him, this affirmation of the absurd by and for their absurdity; pale phantoms that had no faces and no thoughts, they went out looking for something alcoholic to drink, and they had to go to places that were not assigned to North Africans: most of the time to an old miner who sold it to them for its weight in gold, and who made them sign IOUs so that all of them, except Waldik, who kept putting his money aside to buy himself a radio, owed him their salaries months in advance. Those nights, they did not come back to the shack. Drunk with the drunkenness of the damned, they fought one another in the frost, hitting and biting one another, then either laughing or sobbing, convinced that they were not fighting among themselves, but that each and every man was striking out against his life as an outcast. When there was no alcohol—the man they dealt with was shrewd and manipulated the "dosages"—they went back to the shack, lit a candle, and played cards. That was even worse than alcohol, since there was no drunkenness. That meant that the next morning they *remembered:* the same battle, the same rage, the same sobs.

A supervisor fired them all one morning, Waldik because he was coughing and was the type to get tuberculosis—which they wanted to avoid for his sake—the others because they were drunks. Waldik was not upset. By then he had enough money to buy the radio. When he went back, he lifted up the floorboard where he had hidden his money. There was nothing there but an empty box. As for his comrades in misery, they were all gone.

The radio! The days followed one another, one like the other. He had very carefully sorted things out and had only three instincts left:

his stomach, his lodging, and his radio. His stomach had shrunk to a third of normal size, to a third of normal needs, and made its claims only every third day. As for lodging, Waldik learned that you could almost always find something, just like an animal, by relying on instinct: in an old house being demolished or a new building under construction (the essential thing was to go into it late and to leave at dawn); in a vacant house in the suburbs, that had to be staked out and observed, even to the habits of the owners and the probable date of their return. (Some rules of thumb were never to break open a door, never to remove any roof tiles that you couldn't easily replace on departing, and never to turn on any lights or leave any fires.) He'd slept in the hallways of nice apartment buildings on a sofa or on a rug, and he even passed one night in a police van right in front of the precinct station.

He had hung around all kinds of lodgings where you paid: the cellars full of North Africans in Gennevilliers that you went to only when you were completely down and out, places that had no air and no lights and whose inhabitants never went outside—or if they did, they took all sorts of precautions: they had fellow Arabs with knives lie on their mattresses until they got back. Sixty Arabs to a cellar savagely attached to watching what they called their privacy, their property, and their individuality: mattresses as thin as plywood, black and nauseous with filth, covering the whole length of the cellar, and separated from one another by symbolic frontiers as imperious as dogma. Even stooped over, you could hardly imagine people getting in there, but that did not take into account the nature of the inmates. Aside from their function as beds, the mattresses also served as a closet, a table for eating, or for a chamber pot, strewn with a prodigious amount of bric-a-brac, casseroles, empty tin cans, worn clothes, tires, pieces of stale bread . . . Strung from one wall to another in total confusion, strings held up everything that could not go on the beds. To get to one's own and onto it was an art that was innate and could not be learned: you had to know how to leap from the door to the mattress, bent over and not banging against the bric-a-brac hanging on the cords. Otherwise it meant a major battle. Even then you had to know how to stay in your own little space, with the bowlful of air allocated to you, not snoring unless the others snored for quite a while and then snoring along with them, with the same rhythm and the same intensity. If the fleas and bedbugs bit, you couldn't scratch yourself because a simple scratching could bring the whole house of cards tumbling down. Furthermore, it was a waste of time and energy to try to kill those parasites that, like cockroaches and moths, exist in great abundance and are tenacious and lively. Yes indeed! There was an electric lightbulb attached to the ceiling with a theft-proof wiring around it. The Boss turned it off whenever it pleased him, from his lair upstairs. Any other light was strictly forbidden, not by the Boss, who never stepped foot inside the cellars, but by the North Africans themselves: they did not want *to see one another,* to see their own wretchedness. At most, they could put up with a single lightbulb that was as dim, as dirty, and as miserable as they.

These cellars were payable one week in advance, very expensive, hardly less expensive than a room in a cheap hotel—but the Boss counted on the collective sense of the Arabs, who don't want Arabs to live or be seen or die except with Arabs and among Arabs.

And all of those strings! A whole series of hemp cords stretched to breaking point at chin height. Too bad if you were too tall or too short! Just below the cord was a bench. You could sit up on it with your chin resting on the cord. That way you could sleep for an hour, at so much an hour. Time up, a hand slapped the sleeper's shoulder, without any pity.

The radio! He installed it one day in a ruined house where ten Arabs had welcomed him almost with gratitude: they were all old and sick, and he could feed them. He had half bought the radio and half pocketed it from an obese and impotent old man in the back of a store. He pulled up the antenna and plugged it in, dusted it off with his mother's handkerchief and sqatted down. That is all he had wanted for a long, long time. He turned the knobs and chose a voice at random that he recognized with surprise. He modified the tone and turned up the volume. That voice! It was all he could have hoped for! It was the voice of a sheik chanting the Koran. It reminded him that Man had to be worthy of God and assured him that in the eyes of the Sublime Creator he had not suffered; that evil, like suffering, had never existed except in the *human* condition of man, that of all the kingdoms of creation only man had wanted to go beyond his nature as an animal. Thus he was an *unnatural* creature. What we call evil or cruelty in nature, the struggle for survival, illness, death, strong animals eating weaker ones, were, in final analysis, only elements of the Ordering of the World.

But there was something more than words, and he had no need to comprehend. This Koranic incantation went beyond words or ideas or human values. He realized that he was crying. As he realized without looking around that all the other Arabs were crying. Making no noise and shedding no tears, their faces set and their eyes stony: as a tree in a back corner of a building would, or an aging lion in a zoo would cry.

Suddenly down came a fist that broke the charm and the voice, pulled out the wire, and came down again with the cadence of a pylon until the radio was nothing more than scraps of strewn wood and metal.

Waldik stood up. He stood in a vapor and odor of hot blood, and through it he saw the man. He was standing there, gaunt and smiling.

"In my country I'm called Mohammed Ibn Bachir Moussaddik Ould Abou Issa Ibn Abou-El-Mouttalib Ait Ahmed Laaraichi," said the man. "Here they call me Rauss."

His smile grew wider. He was the first Arab Waldik had seen smile since he left Bône.

"You've been to a bad school, old friend! I'm taking you to the Butts."

Waldik followed him.

The motor was coughing and sputtering in the night and the mist.

"You know," said Rauss, "two months ago . . ."

"Yes," said Waldik.

"When I split Simone's shorts in two, don't think I took advantage . . ."

"You should have," bellowed Waldik.

"What?"

"You should have done it."

The other stopped the car and jumped out onto the pavement.

"I'll make up for that right away, damn it!"

"Get back in."

"But since you told me I should have . . ."

"Get back in the car."

Several lights and reflections of lights glimmered on the shimmering pavement. They were the simple, fleeting impressionist reverberations of a dismal landscape. Not a policeman, not the hair of a dog, not even a gray and dirty garbage can could be made out in the murk. A little later on the first startling gleams of a stillborn day, with neither heart nor soul, would make all of its hideousness disappear in one clean sweep. A crow's food! Redemption!

They got out and parked the jalopy behind an empty truck garage.

A good twenty veteran Scapegoats came out and surrounded them. They were the ones who had been through fifteen or twenty years of unemployment and bad temper. No one said a word. They barely coughed. They even spit in silence. They fingered cigarette butts as thin as matchsticks and breathed on their fingers. They had no age or sex. They were dressed in gray and mist, indistinguishable from the distress that surrounded them, and perceptibly separate and distinct only when a cigarette glowed.

"Here's Waldik!" announced Rauss. "He's back."

They were alone, stretched out on a pile of sacks. "Stolen yesterday," said Rauss. "You know how I know? I stole them."

Night was coming outside and in their bones as though it would never go away. The shadow of an Arab appeared, preceded by a scent of boiled carrion. He tossed them a piece of sheep's tail, about three vertibrae long, gamey from the start and rotted by the cooking.

Waldik said he wasn't hungry. The shadow of the Arab that had come out of nowhere, like a guardian angel or a convict's guard, quickly grabbed the meat away from him and began to chew on it.

He could hear the clack of teeth and the chewing until he finally fell asleep. And even in sleep, the sounds invaded him—powerful, mechanical, as though produced by a pack of wolves crouching around a scrawny rabbit, thirty or forty of them tearing at it and chewing it in the night, in the desolate stretches of ice and cold where there would be a rabbit every six months, but where there was cold, ice, and desolation in abundance.

5

Waldik spent the winter with the Butts. He hardly ever spoke to them, and they paid no attention to him.

Sometimes Rauss would seize his friend's face in his two hands and turn it toward the oil lamp. He would examine it for a long time, holding it with his knotty fingers, his gaze fixed and his breathing almost stopped. His desire to understand was like something cruel, born of indecision and a determination to comprehend. Was this the face of a hangman or a saint? He would stick his hands into his pockets and go out to his jalopy that started up like the noise of a heavy head cold.

Sometimes when he was bent over Waldik like that late at night, he would look at him in the cigarette's glow, trying to perceive in his face or in his breathing some betrayal of blemish, an aging cell, or the hypothetical eventuality of a tear. He searched minutely, almost amorously, until finally the cigarette butt would burn down so far that it would singe his lips. When that would happen, he would go outside to urinate into the thick layer of ice, leaving a black, smoking hole. At least the ice showed some reaction. He would come back in, reeling with cold and bumping against the moldy walls of the shack, but mechanically avoiding stepping on the sleeping bodies, pick up the old tarpaulin that he had padded with rags, unlace his shoes without taking them off, then fall asleep like someone hit by a sledge hammer, his chin against his knees.

The cold crackled, the ice hardened, and the bitter winter wind whistled wickedly. It was the evil of the wind to be so cold, reduced to something shrunken and cutting, the wind that in its very essence called for space and plenitute, and now did nothing more than sweep away the jerky breathing and the chattering of bones and teeth of a group of Arabs curled up like sleeping dogs, the squeaking of rusty corrugated iron and odors that already evaporated and already solidified, dusts frozen and tolling out their hunger and future miseries, as weighty in measure and intensity as those of yesterday or of yesteryear. That particular wind may not have originally been cold. It may have had nothing hatefully cutting in its beginnings, like the police (no comment) or laws conceived with fitting compunction and then never enforced. It may simply have encountered some twenty Arabos lying body to body in its path, their breath merging, their teeth chattering, the distress of their bodies even worse than that of their souls (souls that collaborated in forgetting the term 'distress' and that now helped to forget the term for body, what I would designate as rejoicing), neither dead nor alive, hybrid even in the odor that they themselves had whetted, acidified, and brought to a halt in their oxydized corrugated iron for a whole generation of nights.

The awakening was tragic. In the cluster, one Arabo was stirring. He rose to his feet like a phantom and slipped bones, skin, and blood into the frost. The heap broke up like a stack of firearms, with the whining of slaughtered dogs, snortings, the sound of bone against bone, and cursing. Then shaking their heads, their eyes dead, and with their hands trying to move their jaws, the irregular, convulsive pendulum in bone (not even in bone: in pumice stone) of a clock that was a swaying skeleton on which no moustache trembled with the dignity of a double tuft. They were all sitting around the man who had gotten to his feet. For a minute, they stayed there, not even conscious of being awake, like a ship floundering in a sea of ice with one mast standing tall and stiff.

The days did not go by. There was no succession of days and nights. There were only simple temporal sequences like the snapping of a twig or the killing of a louse. Noise grew in intensity but had no meaning, led to nothing precise or determined. One group of Arabs arrived and another left. They had no place in time or space, no shadow and, it would almost seem, no material substance. *Projection in the past,* thought Waldik, *and then even this past was projected toward a misty antiquity, peopled with shadows and echoes.*

Sometimes a hairy hand—an assemblage of fingers, the scaffolding of a house left in a state of scaffold on which had grown some meager grass, some hair—would open, and before it closed again, Waldik would snatch from it a piece of bone covered with a thin layer of meat, or simply a coating of rancid and dubious grease. Sometimes. Ten times a day or every three days, and then it depended on a multitude of factors: predisposition, the cops, laziness, the cold . . .

Rauss explained to him that the scant supply was due to the cold. He was having the Butts hibernate. Normally not a day went by without laying hands on something in a grocery near the Seine. Rauss told him that one night even the Corporal and the Scapegoats had stolen a butcher's truck parked by the central market. They had driven it up to Nanterre as fast as they could and unloaded it piece by piece in the space of a few Koranic prayers. By dawn everything saleable had been negotiated with a fence and the money all drunk up, buried in some lot, or sent off to the villages of North Africa to take care of the clan. As for the meat—six steers—it lasted two full days.

To them, Waldik was a Christian. He tried—and Rauss seconded him—to explain to them why he wanted to expose their miseries in the form of a book: explained that a book was a kind of folded newspaper of some three hundred pages that would be completely devoted to telling their story. One of them shrugged his shoulders—a periodic twitch. They said nothing about their dignity as wounded pariahs. To express it or understand it would have seemed a weakness to them. At most, they cited the case of the guinea-pigs of the house in Nanterre and went right on treating him like a Christian.

Waldik digested their criticisms the way he digested their half-gnawed bones. He went on observing their way of life with the heart-broken indifference of a man brought to a halt. Sometimes, however, a memory of the past, in the form of a quarrel, would come to him. He would raise his head and lean on his elbow against the piece of rubber tire that served as his pillow.

Someone had poured water into the lamp to make the oil rise, then stood close by him and watched him attentively. Another fellow had found some pieces of playing cards. A touch game got under way with heavy betting: a she-camel, a plot of ground that the old folks would bequeath some day in the distant future, a war, and everybody was back in the Middle Ages; betting a sister and a mother, or at least whatever could be stolen once this damned winter was over. The thin smoking flame of the lamp lowered and sputtered and danced, quivering like their voices and their verbal fevers that rose all of a sudden as they fidgeted on a space of the floor where spitting and blows and cursing and bodies hitting and drunken laughter all melted together. Then just as quickly there was silence except for the snoring of those who, like a Booz from the century of steel, were sleeping. Through it all, Waldik, transformed into a pair of eyes, watched and reflected: *they no doubt have never lived;* reflected: *lived fully with hopes and desires and inhibitions.*

They had even been unemployed. With bursts of laughter they recalled the time in their lives when they had had unemployment cards that they had to have punched on a certain day so they could collect an unemployment benefit. They were still amazed by it. Some of them had even received letters from their native village, to which they sent a part of the money, a village in a holiday mood: the Christians pay our sons not to do any work! They had a devil of a time keeping their family from coming up to join them, women, children, cousins, and friends. Now, however, it was only a fairy tale good for filling in an evening's conversation by the light of the oil lamp. The eldest of the group, the Corporal, provided with a long string of official papers, had been unemployed for ten whole years.

One night Waldik woke up with a start.

There was a sudden bustling about like the eve of a holiday. An Arabo put his fingers to his lips. Sh! Someone had found a guidebook and everyone had a right to say something, under the chairmanship of the Corporal.

"Rome," said one.

"Damacus," said another.

"New York," chimed in a third.

New York! The very name symbolized a grand parade of Buicks stuffed with corned beef and dollars. He could see it with conviction, with force, penetration and details, so well that Waldik, sitting down at present, turned the piece of tire over and over in his hands. They were all leaving the next day for New York. The train would leave at 6:02. There was a wait of about three hours in Le Havre for registering baggage, for customs and passport inspection. They waved those passports like excited dwarfs under the lamp light, passed them from hand to hand, and outdid one another in going over the nameless problems in getting a visa. One thing was certain: the Queen Mary raised anchor at 2 P.M. Then followed a moment of meditation, almost of fervor, during which every stone and every piece of board was given its last farewell. After that the "valises" had to be packed—paper bags and cardboard boxes into which even Waldik's piece of tire and the rags he was sitting on were stuffed with cries of glee.

It was only due to his reflexes that Wakdik was not reduced to a pulp. He jumped up and in two leaps was at the threshhold. Inside, arms and legs tangled together, knives gleamed and glowed late into the night, and without a single cry or complaint the multiform and barbaric fighters struggled on, goaded by that idiot dream that they had just dreamed in common, the dream of a voyage that they had never made and of a freedom that they would never know.

Waldik was an observer, not a participant. The monotony of it all kept him awake and alert—as though he were waiting for some kind of variation, some kind of theme as yet undeveloped.

One night he told them with sobs in his voice that he had come back to France only for them, that they should cry out, revolt, do anything other than squat there . . . He rose to his feet and went about kissing each one's hand. That night too the same Arabo shrugged the same shoulders.

"Something like a diploma?" began the Corporal. "We've got some graduates here."

Indeed there were some escapees and even one man who had been condemned to death. He had fasted for a full month, and that had completely changed the structure of his face. He had held the tips of his fingers to a live coal until the digital point was cooked away. Then he changed his name from Ahmed ben Hamed to Hamed ben Ahmed.

They were suspicious of words, of dreams, and of ideologies. They had all been sentenced for something, from crimes of common law to crimes of opinion. All except one quiet old man who never slept, never ate, and drank now and then a gallon of a liquid that gave off the scent of fermented apples. When he drank it he would bark like a police dog. Papers, he would howl, hurry up! . . . into the cell . . . Next one! . . .

The winter became hallucinating. Even the wind had moved on some time before, and it had not snowed for quite a while. It was a winter reduced to its simplest element, and its most ferocious: a cold that had the silent force of a block of ice. Sleep went on forever. Sometimes it lasted for two days.

Now only Rauss went outside, and no one understood how the motor of his jalopy didn't freeze up. Rauss would smile, invoke the name of Allah, and spit on his hands. The four hardened wheels started up, wheels that followed the same two ruts to the last millimeter, like a train on a pair of rails, an atavistic ancestral habit of mechanical engines like those patriarchs of Africa vigorously burying their fourth or fifth descendants and which defied every law of atmosphere, physics, or even of human speculation.

He came back over the same road late at night with his headlights out. It took half a dozen arms and several hours of effort to get the motor stopped. It seemed to go right on defying the man who had gotten it started and even, you might say, the man, long since turned to mineral, who had conceived it. It coughed and shook with fits of laughter.

Rauss threw some sticks on a piece of burning paper and put his hands to the fire; then he pointed out in a loud voice the corner in which he had stowed the "merchandise." The sticks flamed up all of a sudden, revealing a powerful play of jawbones but not waking up the sleepers: all you had to do was tap them on the chin and they gobbled up and chewed away without so much as opening an eye.

On those nights, Waldik did not sleep. He waited until the breathing was even and there was no danger. Then he would go out to join Rauss in a landscape of ice and there, shivering, gaunt and somber, would chew with rage what Rauss called dessert: usually the only piece of meat that he had been able to steal, and what he had held back for him.

They hardly ever talked to each other. Or, to be more exact, after days of silence, Waldik would say, in an unsteady voice, such idiocies as: "Spring won't be long in coming to life again . . ."

Rauss would not reply. He would offer him a cigarette and quietly watch him smoke it, with a curiosity that combined pity and bitterness.

"Isn't that right? We're all going to come to life again," said Waldik.

He snuffed out the cigarette with the tips of his two fingers and stuffed the butt in his pocket.

Then he would repeat:

"Come to life again! . . ."

One night he saw him come in walking quickly, saying that he would wait behind the shack with an open can of sardines.

"Wine! Find me a bottle of wine . . ."

The next day he brought him one. Waldik put it under his arm, and Rauss watched him walk down one of the ruts in the road. He did not come back until the next day. In his eyes there was no sign of recognition.

He flopped down and went to sleep. Several days later, he asked Rauss for another bottle. Then the requests became frequent. He would walk out into the night, haggard, with eyes that were lifeless and a voice full of cruelty, shouting that he wanted a bottle of wine.

Then he would go off with the wine under his arm, down the length of the path that the two ruts formed, almost in the same tracks he had traced before, neither hurriedly nor feverishly, until he was nothing more than an abject spot in a vast stretch of desolation.

One night Rauss refused to give him anything.

"I won't give you this bottle until you tell me where you go, what you do, and what catastrophe you're preparing for the two of us and for all the rest."

His voice was clear, incisive, free of all pity. Waldik understood very well, and suddenly knelt down in front of him.

"I don't want to love," he cried. "I don't want to love her . . . I don't want to love any more . . . Even if she were a pure woman, even if she were nothing like the one who threw me out . . . Drink, I need a drink . . . I want to drink and destroy in myself any hope of redemption and go on being just an Arabo . . ."

PART THREE

NIHIL OBSTAT

1

The first time Simone noticed the bottle of wine, she came to no conclusions. At most she smiled indulgently—an expression of good will.

Now she sat watching to door every night. She had been advised to complain to the police, but she would not listen. She hadn't even heard.

When the door opened, she immediately saw the bottle of red wine, and she began to tremble.

Waldik never came with any regularity. When he left, he gave her a military salute and nothing more. He walked out as silently as he entered. It was at night that he came. It was in the morning that Simone could sleep. The same person who had advised her to make a complaint suggested that she lock her door or get a watchdog. Simone did nothing. The real danger would have been precisely in such useless precautions.

The door would open and in he would come. He would break open the bottle against the wall without ever breaking more than the neck and leaving the bottle intact. Then he would go toward the bed where Simone sat trembling. It was always the same hallucinatory slow approach, the same brusque halt several feet away from her, and the same exchange of retorts—like a scene that she had played a hundred times over and that she would do over and over again without any desire to do so, a role forced on her that locked her into a tight and burdensome armor, abolishing life and taking its place. She could not even hate any more.

"Are you thirsty?"

"No, thank you."

"How is Fabrice?"

"Hardly any better."

"Ah!"

Memory recalled, even before the series of acts abated. A long time afterwards, memory pitilessly recaptured the most minute details and filled in the empty moments between two series of acts, as though precisely the continuance of the nightmare was born from the simple fact, from the simple desire to forget, from a simple indifference.

She had covered the lightbulb with a shade made from a piece of napkin. He tore off the shade with a single twist of the broken bottle, then wrapped the cloth around the bottle like a halo. He looked into her eyes.

"You aren't thirsty?"

"No, thank you."

"Ah!"

She watched the bottle swirl around the room—now, standing on the points of his toes, he sketched out bizarre ballet movements, the bottle following along, synthesizing the rhythms, perched high on the end of his outstretched arm and still with its aureole of cloth.

The movement became so rapid for a moment that everything seemed to have ceased: a dark silhouette twisting like a corkscrew, a pair of shoes that seemed nailed at the toe to the floor like footwear on display in a shop window. She was no longer trembling. She was thinking: *I am that bottle of wine. As if he were turning my imponderable brain matter. At the end of his arm and I let him do it, and I can only accept it quietly.* She thought: *instinct face to face with madness.*

"You are thirsty!"

"No, I tell you."

"You *should* be thirsty."

"No, no . . . NO!"

But they were paltry interjections. She closed her mouth as firmly as she crossed her legs, a row of teeth forming a rampart to the former, and if she could have put two rows around her legs, she would have. A Goridan knot, while he seemed to spring and leap and become a bottle beside her, or a hand, two eyes.

Much later on, after she had washed all traces of wine or the smell of wine from her skin, her clothes, the sheets, and the floor, she opened the dictionary to look up the word "wine." She wanted to know its etymology, its definition, and its usage . . . All she found was a little hole in the shape of a rectangle. With her own hand, the day after the first bottle had appeared, she had cut out the section WINE with a razor blade. A miniscule piece of paper that she had burned and whose ashes she had carefully interred.

She shut the book with a bang: I must have dreamed all that. Mortified by the thought that she had no doubt only dreamed it. Old Josepha and other neighbors watched her grow thinner, as day by day she became more amorphous.

"Meningitis lasts a long time . . . but your child will come back to you. Don't be upset."

She was mortified to hear these old women's voices, to recognize that they had probably come because of the child. One of them had lent her a sewing machine, and they vied with one another in skill, digging up outmoded and moth-eaten old dresses, lingerie from the 1900's, and pieces of cloth and lace out of an old trunk. They all tried to explain their ideas: how to make a pair of short pants with buttons at the knees for a boy, or how to make a cap out of a piece of underwear.

They stayed there. Knitting and chatting, listening to the grinding and groaning of the sewing machine, they were thinking: *If only she would go away! If only it would occur to her to sell her little house, at half price, and leave without even saying goodbye!*

They were bent over their needles and handiwork, and from one woman to another went a language of their own, click, click . . . of course, you're quite right . . . Click, click . . . I saw him on the steps last night like some kind of ghost . . . Click, click . . . I heard cursing, I tell you . . . I didn't shut an eye all night long . . . click, click . . .

It was Josepha who first opened fire. Late one afternoon she stuck her knitting needles into a ball of yarn, and with a decided gesture adjusted her spectacles and said:

"We can't go along any longer . . . none of us (they all nodded their heads in perfect agreement) can stand these things any longer. We don't know whether you are happy about it or if you're going crazy. One thing's certain, and it's this: we are going to save you in spite of that madman."

The heads all nodded complete agreement! Simone handed them their things without saying a word.

They left somewhat disconcerted, their hands stuck into their shabby dresses as if they were muffs. Their nostrils steamed in the cold air. She really is crazy, but we'll save her anyway. Indeed!

The sound of their steps faded into the distance. *Now,* thought Simone, *I'll be alone and there will be no tomorrow.* Mechanically she pushed back a curl that kept falling on her forehead. She looked haggard and exhausted. *Even their hands, their sure and sugary smell, taking comfort in the old clothes that I took apart, that I sewed together again—I won't even have that bone to pick.*

Suddenly she pushed the pedal and the machine began to whir, snorting and jerking faster and faster. The thread jumped out of the needle, and the needle itself snapped crazily. The pedal rose and fell more and more dizzily until both woman and machine were fused into a single outcry: I-am-crazy . . . I-am-crazy . . . I-am-crazy . . .

When spring came, Rauss knew.

One morning he hit him over the head with the bottle, threw him into the jalopy and started off. When the car came to a stop, Isabelle was standing behind the garden gate, tall, thin, very young, and with two spots of light where her eyes should have been.

"Is he there?" she asked.

"He sure is!" said Rauss.

He took Waldik on his shoulder and tossed him into the garden on the other side of the fence.

"I'm sick and tired of this guy," he yelled. "And the Butts are sick of him too. He still thinks he's their prophet! And Simone's sick of him and the Placement Bureaus and the prisons and the Settlement House at Nanterre and Mac O'Mac and the priests and every Christian in the country. I'm going to tell you something. It won't be long before you'll be sick of him too. Greetings!"

Off he went in his jalopy that fit him like a suit of clothes. He left so quickly that later on Isabelle had the impression that he turned the car around with a simple twist of the wrist. Yes, she said to herself, even Rauss is down on him now.

She helped him to his feet and hardly recognized him. He had let his beard grow: *just like a saint,* he must have thought; *just like a tramp,* she thought.

That foggy morning that she had helped him when she found him drunk in the street, she had not thought of pity. She gave him a hand and led him over to a bench. He told her about Simone and about his son, about Mac, his parents, his homeland, the Arabos, the Butts, Rauss, and about what he was writing and his disillusionments. She listened to him, but felt no pity. She did not even know what pity was, nor the difference between good and evil. Her conception of the world was quite simple; a man is equal to a flower, and the world is an immense flower garden. She never philosophized. She believed what she had been taught by family, teachers, books and experience, and was the sum total of trial and error.She believed that it was not of the world that she should expect her substance and her life, but that it was up to her, up to every human being (as with trees, animals, birds and flowers) to *give* their life to the world—I must open my flesh and surrender myself, she would say. She was neither enlightened nor arrogant: she *was,* and that was all. Not one single time did she ever look someone straight in the eye without, as she would put it, scratching away the surface, the mask, and without leaving the person troubled and naked. She believed in the goodness and the fundamental vitality of man.

She listened to Waldik and was convinced that if society had made a derelict of him (or as he put it, with pitiable pride, a diagram, a cancer), he also had his part in it in cowardly and resounding measure.

"Come," she said simply.

They both got up. Slender and with the delicacy and weight—and the mixture of audacity and of umbrage—of a bird, he grasped her by the waist and with her in the hollow of his arm crossed streets and intersections and roads. Later on they would remember that their feet had taken wing.

"You are very proud," she said. "You are very egotistical. You've never wanted to be anything but ego and pride."

He did not move. It was evening. He was satisfied, washed, and relaxed. They were both sitting in Isabelle's bedroom. A stove stoked with coke was snorting and smoking slightly. In front of them, a curtainless window cut across the branches of leafless trees against an opening of mauve horizon and patches of snow on black earth.

He did not move, only his hands . . . *My hands!,* he thought. *If I closed them on her waist, I would hear the cracking of a bird's bones.*

"If you thought I brought you here out of charity," she added, "or because my body demands something exotic or because what is unwholesome attracts me, you are wrong."

She grabbed his head in her hands.

"It's strange," she said, "when things are so old, they give you chills. How old are you?"

He struck her.

Later that night, she was drowsily quiet and naked in his arms. She would never grow old and never die—unless he killed her. Compared to her childhood, the miseries of an Arabo were only the scab on the wound. Before going to sleep, she talked to him about the war, about the Nazi occupation and the exodus from Paris, about the crumbs of black bread that she survived on as a child. About men's madness that had taken her father from her, taken the calcium of her body. Now, some ten years after the Liberation, she was still, and always would be, nothing more than a skeleton with decalcified teeth, with fingernails that split off in winter, and half a dozen muscles the size of a pidgeon's. THERE WAS NOTHING SHE HAD TO PARDON ANYONE FOR. When she saw those children born of the war, empty, without faith, without ideals, she wondered if they weren't offspring of the Germans—or larvae that the Nazis had carefully scattered over the soil of France, with clear purpose and a Machiavellian calculation as though to show that France would never have anything else but young people like that.

In the tenuous light of the nightlamp, Waldik examined his left hand. It was the hand that had struck her. He looked at it with astonishment, as though it did not belong to him. He did not want to cry or to weaken. He simply jumped out of bed, saw a table with a marble top, and hit it. He hit not the marble, but the hand that had dared to touch that woman who was thinner and purer than his mother. He hit it deliberately, methodically, as though he were counting out the blows, until his hand was nothing more than a numb and heavy lump.

He sat down in the garden. That was where he was sitting at present, pounding the earth with his two hands in memory of that night that, had he so wished, could have had a dawn. His own. An important one.

When he stopped striking the earth, she helped him get up. During all that time, she had remained standing beside him, but she had been careful not to interfere. She kept telling herself that perhaps by beating his hands black and blue, he would finally go beyond suffering. *Yes,* she thought, *if dogs can go beyond the fate of being the dogs that men have made of them, keeping them shut up and showing them so much affection, they would turn into wolves— or rather, remembering what Man has done to them, they would walk Them on leashes.*

What he did was to get up and look at her. He was weak no longer.

"All I wanted," he said, "was to avoid dying a second time. I don't trust love any more than misery, and I hate it. I don't want to love again . . . love already killed me once."

"No," she said, "you aren't through yet. From the beginning, you have seen yourself as someone who was sacrificed. Look at Rauss, for God's sake! Think about him. Even if for years now everyone has been saying and writing and printing that truth does not exist, we have *our own* truth. Tell me, when you left Algeria again, was it because you couldn't stand the look in the eyes of your brothers? Because they could not recognize you any more?"

"Be quiet . . . be quiet . . ."

"Yes," she went on, "those strands of sea-weed that you call a beard, that redemption based on sadism, those hands of a murderer—don't you know that even Rauss has no use for you any longer? And you're still talking about the soul! . . ."

She shook him, opened the gate, and pushed him outside.

"The exploitation of Arabs by Europeans, yes," she said emphatically with a bitter laugh. "I do condemn them, those people who drove you from your homes, who don't know what to do with you, and don't even have pity on you. Yes, I can take sides, generalize, and recognize that our civilization makes you despair. Yes, I am ashamed to be European, but it is you North Africans yourselves that I condemn the most. You have always let yourselves be exploited, and you have always been exploited. Long before the French got to you, you were nothing more than bastards that everybody passed from one to the other, generation after generation, century after century, like a plot of ground: Phoenicians, Greeks, Romans, Visigoths, Vandals, Arabs, Turks, French . . ."

"Shut up," he yelled.

'No, I won't. If I shut up, it would be to condemn myself too and to admit that I was wrong not to be happy to be a larva. It would destroy my pride. But try to understand me," she cried, standing face to face with him, "that when I picked you up in the street, I didn't see your misery. I really don't know what misery is. If you talk to me about old clothes and rags, about greasy skin and that beard, about a stomach pitted with hunger and unemployment, no, that's not misery. That is all physical, all temporal, and has no importance whatsoever. Your misery is of the soul. No Frenchman, and no sum total of history created it in you. It comes from you alone. You will die with it. You live more like a prisoner of it than in any jail, more sadistically than in a hairshirt, and oh, so very contented! When I picked you up in the street, I wanted only to see the man in you. I made a mistake. There was no man in you. I picked up a piece of rag, and now I'm throwing that rag away."

She walked away, shivering and exhausted. She already knew.

He grabbed hold of her hand and took her in his arms. There was such an affection in him that she pressed against him.

"The Butts," he said in a hoarse voice, "go see the Butts. Do you want me to take you to see them? Go see them first. Then you can do what you want."

Two holes of light closed over two tears. She gently pulled herself away from him.

"Let's go," she said softly. "But do you think it's necessary? Do you think they can do anything for you . . . for . . ."

She added nothing more: *and for our love.* Because she already knew. *Why,* she thought, *why in the name of God aren't I a larva too? Everything would be so much simpler . . .*

2

When the thrush sang, there was a mad scramble to get outside.

Sitting in a circle at the entrance to their corrugated shack, nodding their heads and swaying back and forth with the regularity of a pendulum, the Butts clapped their hands and recited strange passages of psalmodic verse. Only the Corporal and the old policeman were not chanting. One was playing a string-instrument and another a kind of xylophone. No one, not even they, not even a Christian who might have passed by (the neighborhood where the Butts lived was reputedly dangerous, so no one passed by) would have risked saying, on hearing the sounds they produced, that instead of a string-instrument and a xylophone, what they were playing on was a rusty casserole attached to a rusty bicycle wheel whose spokes were chords, and a flatiron set on the side of a brick that was played by hitting it with two big nails.

Of course they weren't songs at all, nor psalmodic verses, nor even a human sound produced by a human voice. You might describe them at best as the gutteral echoes of some savage battle between a wild beast and a prehistoric man in a prehistoric cave. But there had been the song of the thrush, and that was what was important.

In the center of the Butts there were three stakes. They had been hurriedly stuck in the ground and connected one to another by a piece of wire. On the wire they had hung what had once been an animal, or what they imagined had been a sheep that had been skinned and cleaned and that was roasting in what was more smoke than flame from a thin wisp of wood fire. It was the Corporal who had taken charge of the business. With a single stroke of the razor, without even taking time to fully open it up, he faced the east and cut the ruminant's throat: he was an expert at such things, and it was as though he had slaughtered a man. Then he had skinned it, but so rapidly that along with the fleece he had cut away pieces of skin and meat, and even a vertebra. He hadn't completely cleaned it out. The small intestines and the spleen could be eaten. All of that time the Butts remained squatting, mentally reciting prayers that spoke of succulent meat. They watched as their tongues licked their moustaches, like wolves to whom one would talk of Abraham's sacrifice. When the Corporal got to his feet, the fleece had disappeared, and there was not a trace of blood.

The thrush had been singing since dawn. That was when they knew it was spring. Every spring on the same day, at almost the same minute, it would sing, both distant and near, invisible and almost incorporeal. They would rush out of their cubbyhole of oxydized metal, get undressed, wash themselves and redress, laughing and shouting with broad gestures as though all of space belonged to them, and all the vast future and a full and ardent life. Winter was dead, and the cold was buried in the earth. At least they vaguely remembered having gone hungry just like their brothers in Africa with only one difference, primarily a verbal one, that for the latter was the ritual of a month of fasting that Islam calls Ramadan, and that for them, the Butts, were long months of winter and hibernation.

They recalled that things were not always that way. The song of the thrush began the festival of sacrifice in their distant villages where they had perhaps been born in a past immemorial of which they no longer had any knowledge, not even in name. All they retained—alive and eternal within them—was the song of the thrush.

All of the holidays in Algeria began in the same way. There was the festival of sacrifice, the festival of water, the gathering of dates and the harvest, the tilling and the sewing, circumcision, birth and death. A Kabyle man would pick up the cornemuse in his hands and play the song of the thrush. Strangely enough, the thrush was always there, singing exactly at the time it should, as if Mohammed in person had placed it there to remind them that they were and always would be slaves to the Law and the Book, and that whether civilizations decayed or stood, the Book and the Law would endure. The circle of Butts, sitting around on the ground clapping their hands, with voices like bulldozers or automatic drills, chanted verses of a modernized Koran in which it was a question of the bone of the earth transformed by man into cement and of man transformed into reinforced concrete. Their chants were like those songs of initiation and African sorcery that passed through European civilization to give birth to jazz, but with the difference that, in the case of the Butts it was jazz that was transformed into sorcery.

Each of them watched the mutton cooking as though he were watching Mohammed himself, and each one deep inside realized that this was not just a ritual that was reborn in this way every year, but their very flesh, their organs, their instincts, and their thirst for life: like a marmot after the winter, or trees that die in winter and burst forth in spring. They followed the same rhythm as the earth and knew that the miseries, bad tempers, hatreds, hunger, and cruelty of man were as necessary as pruning and cutting trees, as useful as poverty or death—but it was essential to attribute to them their justice and precise value. They had always limited themselves to that. Man's mission is to avoid being destroyed.

Many a winter had chilled their bones, but they had never enlarged or intensified their sufferings to the dimensions of a law. The only conclusion they had drawn was the recognition that in all times and in all places there had always been men—and not just North Africans in France—whose fate it was to be sacrificial victims, whether the Negro in America, the Jew in the Middle East, the Moslem in India, the slaves of ancient Rome or Greece, unassimilated into a civilization, as though to prove that no creation of man has ever been for everyone or ever been perfect.

Their circumstances as sacrificial victims should have gladdened them, as the Butts rejoiced in themselves, twenty-two North Africans of the 300,000 in France, they alone who had comprehended the opportunity that had been granted to them to utilize their misery as one would a knife. They had, in effect, used it that way, cutting themselves away from everything that could link them to man, to the past, to the future, or to the life of man, and instinctively going back in time to the sources of creation to become again plain creatures of God in the natural state of creature, hibernating in winter, being reborn in spring, stealing their food, with rusty shacks for their lodging, with a language that expressed their needs and their instincts, static like their truck garage or Rauss's jalopy, with no evolution except the aging of cells, killing all hope in them, the pure and chimerical creation that man only created because he wanted to go beyond his condition as creature, and thus become a misfit on the earth.

The Butts clapped their hands and chanted. The only thing of their past as men that they remembered was the song of the thrush.

When the last ember had gone out, they knew that the sheep was cooked. Knife blades glimmered and cut the meat with cries of joy. They all got up and danced in a circle. No, they had not suffered. No, there had never been a winter.

When Rauss's jalopy came to a stop, there was nothing left but a hoof hanging from a stake, but Isabelle got out, gnawed on it, and joined their dance. Not a single eye saw her as a woman. When the Corporal saw her, he raised an arm, and the circle formed around her and went on dancing. Even Waldik recognized that now there were twenty-three Butts.

They danced late into the night. They had lit another wood fire, but the second one was a big one and crackled noisily. They would leap over it with cries of delight, and when it went down, a piece of something flammable, a tire or a box, a carton or a bit of lumber, would come out of nowhere from no one, and onto the pile it would go. The fire would start up again, and the dance would resume its rhythm.

Late into the night, almost at dawn, the thrush sang a second time. It always sang a second time at every festival as if to signify that everything in this world, even life, had an ending.

Several embers were smoking, and several bones of the roasted animal, eaten and digested and already calcified, that had once been a sheep. Isabelle shook hands with everyone. She had no need to say anything.

When it came to the Corporal's turn, he shook her hands with his own bat-like hands. She made no complaint. The strength of them could have come from the hands of a monkey.

"Take him away," he said in a breath. "Take him away with you and give him children and a home and the stability of a civilized man.

That is what he has tended toward, and what he's always wanted. Nothing else."

She looked into his eyes. They were sunken so deeply into their orbits that the brows looked like the visor of a cap. *Yes,* she thought, *as if to protect oneself from life.*

"All I possess," he added, "is this rusty shack. I'd gladly sell it . . . to help you. What the devil! There are caves around here."

They looked for Rauss for quite a while. It was only after the sun came up that they found him, peacefully asleep under his jalopy. He never had been an Arabo.

3

A little Arab boy was shining shoes in the Algerian city of Bône. The shoes were black, and they belonged to a priest.

"What's your name?" asked the priest.

"Yalaan Waldik," said the Berber.

"What do you do, and how old are you, my child?"

"I am a shoeshine boy, and I'm ten years old."

The priest sighed.

"In ten years, I will be a shoeshine boy twenty years old, if God so wills."

The priest got angry.

"Just think, my child," he said, "if you were in France, you would already be learning Latin and Greek, and in ten years you would be a man."

The little Berber boy looked at him, stupified. For the first time, he calculated, reckoned, and speculated. Then he closed his shoeshine box as one closes the door to the past, and he went out on his way. He persuaded his father to sell his last goat by telling him that with the price of this single goat he could buy him a thousand, in ten year's time. And he left for France.

The priest said aloud: "I have saved a soul."

POSTFACE

The question has been asked me, and I have asked it of myself, if I am capable now twenty years later of writing such a book, one equally atrocious. It is hard for me to answer, except with another question: does racism still exist in France twenty years later? Are the immigrants who continue to come to work in this "so highly civilized" country still penned up on the edges of society and humankind? Is it still true, as my master Albert Camus stated, that the bacillus of the plague never dies and never disappears?

D.C.
Ile d'Yeu, France
July 17th, 1976